Terry Pratchett was born in 1948 and is still not dead. He started work as a journalist one day in 1965 and saw his first corpse three hours later, work experience *meaning* something in those days. After doing just about every job it's possible to do in provincial journalism, except of course covering Saturday afternoon football, he joined the Central Electricity Generating Board and became press officer for four nuclear power stations. He'd write a book about his experiences if he thought anyone would believe it.

All this came to an end in 1987 when it became obvious that the Discworld series was much more enjoyable than real work. Since then the books have reached double figures and have a regular place in the bestseller lists. He also writes books for younger readers. Occasionally he gets accused of literature.

Terry Pratchett lives in Wiltshire with his wife Lyn and daughter Rhianna. He says writing is the most fun anyone can have by themselves.

Stephen Briggs was born in Oxford in 1951 and he still lives there, with his wife Ginny and their sons, Philip and Christopher.

In what would generally pass for real life he works for a small government department dealing with the food industry. However, as an escape to a greater reality, he has been involved for many years in the machiavellian world of amateur dramatics, which is how he came to discover the Discworld.

Stephen is, by nature, a Luddite, but the Discworld has drawn him into the world of PCs, wordprocessing and electronic mail; he has even been known to paddle on the Internet. His other interests include sketching, back-garden ornithology and Christmas. He has never read *Lord of the Rings* all the way through.

Books by Terry Pratchett

THE COLOUR OF MAGIC*
THE LIGHT FANTASTIC*
EQUAL RITES*
MORT*
SOURCERY*
WYRD SISTERS*
PYRAMIDS*
GUARDS! GUARDS!*
ERIC (co-published with Gollancz)
MOVING PICTURES*
REAPER MAN
WITCHES ABROAD*
SMALL GODS*
LORDS AND LADIES
MEN AT ARMS
SOUL MUSIC
INTERESTING TIMES

THE COLOUR OF MAGIC – GRAPHIC NOVEL
THE LIGHT FANTASTIC – GRAPHIC NOVEL
THE STREETS OF ANKH-MORPORK
(with Stephen Briggs)
THE DISCWORLD MAPP (with Stephen Briggs)
MORT – THE PLAY (adapted by Stephen Briggs)
WYRD SISTERS – THE PLAY
(adapted by Stephen Briggs)

GOOD OMENS (with Neil Gaiman)
STRATA
THE DARK SIDE OF THE SUN

TRUCKERS*
DIGGERS*
WINGS*
THE CARPET PEOPLE
ONLY YOU CAN SAVE MANKIND*
JOHNNY AND THE DEAD*
JOHNNY AND THE BOMB*

*also available in audio

and published by Corgi

THE UNADULTERATED CAT
MORT: A DISCWORLD BIG COMIC
THE DISCWORLD COMPANION
(with Stephen Briggs)
TERRY PRATCHETT'S
DISCWORLD QUIZBOOK
by David Langford

published by Gollancz

TERRY PRATCHETT'S

WYRD SISTERS
the play

adapted for the stage by
STEPHEN BRIGGS

CORGI BOOKS

WYRD SISTERS – THE PLAY
A CORGI BOOK : 0 552 14430 4

First publication in Great Britain

PRINTING HISTORY
Corgi edition published 1996

Wyrd Sisters originally published in Great Britain by
Victor Gollancz Ltd
Copyright © Terry and Lyn Pratchett 1988

Stage adaptation copyright © by
Terry Pratchett and Stephen Briggs 1996

Discworld® is a registered trademark

The right of Terry Pratchett and Stephen Briggs to be identified as the authors of
this work has been asserted in accordance with sections 77 and 78 of the
Copyright Designs and Patents Act 1988.

Set in 12pt Monotype Ehrhardt by
Phoenix Typesetting, Ilkley, West Yorkshire

Corgi Books are published by Transworld Publishers Ltd,
61–63 Uxbridge Road, London W5 5SA,
in Australia by Transworld Publishers (Australia) Pty Ltd,
15–25 Helles Avenue, Moorebank, NSW 2170,
and in New Zealand by Transworld Publishers (NZ) Ltd,
3 William Pickering Drive, Albany, Auckland.

Printed and bound in Great Britain by
Cox & Wyman Ltd, Reading, Berks.

INTRODUCTION

AN AWFULLY BIG ADVENTURE

Since the publication of *The Streets of Ankh-Morpork*, I have been drawn ever further into the Discworld universe. As well as working with Terry on *The Discworld Companion*, I was suddenly in demand – well, OK, I was in demand when I was dressed as *Death* – to pose for publicity photos. The first session was for a Discworld computer game; then Death was again summoned to be photographed with Dave Greenslade and Terry for his CD *From the Discworld*. I was delighted to find myself invited to 'play' Didactylos in the *Small Gods* track; yes, that was me – 'Nevertheless, the Turtle *does* move'. Er . . . not my *real* voice, of course.

Death even got an invitation to London's flashiest Indian restaurant to have a curry with a group of journalists as part of the publicity for a Discworld computer game. A whole room full of journalists but, unfortunately for Death, no take-away.

My drama club has now staged *Wyrd Sisters*, *Mort*, *Guards! Guards!*, *Men at Arms* and *Maskerade*. We were even invited to act out a tiny extract from 'our' *Guards!*

Guards! for Sky TV's Book Programme.

In fact, Oxford's Studio Theatre Club were the first people ever to dramatise the Discworld.

We had a theatre that seats ninety people. We had a stage that was about the size of a pocket handkerchief with the wings of Tinkerbell. Put on a Discworld play? Simple . . .

A flat, circular world borne through space on the backs of four enormous elephants who themselves stand on the carapace of a cosmically large turtle? Nothing to it. A seven-foot skeleton with glowing blue eyes? *No* problem. A sixty-foot fire-breathing dragon? A cinch.

My drama club had already staged its own adaptations of other works: Monty Python's *Life of Brian* and *Holy Grail* – and Tom Sharpe's *Porterhouse Blue* and *Blott on the Landscape*. We were looking for something new when someone said, 'Try Terry Pratchett – you'll like him.'

So I ventured into the previously uncharted territory of the 'Fantasy' section of the local bookstore. I read a Terry Pratchett book; I liked it. I read all of them. I wrote to Terry and asked if we could stage *Wyrd Sisters*. He said yes.

Wyrd Sisters sold out.

So did *Mort* the year after.

So did *Guards! Guards!*, *Men at Arms* and *Maskerade* in the three years after that. In fact, 'sold out' is too modest a word. 'Oversold very quickly so that by the time the local newspaper mentioned it was on we'd had to close the booking office' is nearer the mark.

My casts were all happy enough to read whichever book we were staging, and to read others in the canon too. The books stand on their own, but some knowledge of the wider Discworld ethos helps when adapting the stories, and can help the actors with their characterisations.

The Discworld stories are remarkably flexible in their character requirements. *Mort* has been performed successfully with a cast of three (adding in an extra thrill for the audience, who knew that sooner or later a character would have to have a dialogue with *themselves*. But it turned out very well). On the other hand, there is plenty of scope for peasants, wizards, beggars, thieves and general rhubarb merchants if the director is lucky enough to have actors available.

I'd better add a note of caution here. There are a lot of small parts in the plays which nevertheless require good acting ability (as we say in the Studio Theatre Club: 'There are no small parts, only small actors'). The character may have only four lines to say but one of them might well be the (potentially) funniest line in the play. Terry Pratchett is remarkably democratic in this respect. Spear-carriers, demons and even a humble doorknocker all get their moment of glory. Don't let them throw it away!

Terry writes very good dialogue. Not all authors do. But Terry, like Dickens, writes stuff which you can lift straight into your play. Although it was often necessary to combine several scenes from the book into one scene in the play, I tried to avoid changing the original Pratchett dialogue. After all, you perform an author's work because you like their style; as much of that style as possible should be evident in the play.

We aimed to keep our adaptations down to about two hours running time – with a 7.30 start and allowing twenty minutes for an interval, that would get the audience into the pub for an after-play drink by about 9.50, with the cast about ten minutes after them (although slower-moving members of the audience might well find the cast already propping up the bar – we are true Coarse Actors!). Also, two hours is about right for the average play. This of course meant that some difficult decisions had to be taken in order to boil down the prose.

The important thing was to decide what was the basic plot: anything which didn't contribute to that was liable to be dropped in order to keep the play flowing. Favourite scenes, even favourite characters, had to be dumped.

I had to remember that not all the audience would be dyed-in-the-wool Pratchett fans. Some of them might just be normal theatre-goers who'd never read a fantasy novel in their whole lives, although I have to say that these now are a dwindling minority.

The books are episodic, and this can be a difficult concept to incorporate into a play. Set changes slow down the action. Any scene change that takes more than thirty seconds means you've lost the audience. Even *ten*-second changes, if repeated often enough, will lead to loss of interest.

The golden rule is – if you can do it without scenery, do it without scenery. It's a concept that has served radio drama very well (everyone *knows* that radio has the best scenery). And Shakespeare managed very well without it, too.

The plays do, however, call for some unusual props. Many of these were made by the cast and crew: a door with a hole for a talking, golden doorknocker, coronation mugs, large hourglasses for Death's house, sponge chips and pizzas, shadow puppets, archaic rifles, dragon-scorched books and Discworld newspapers ('Patrician Launches Victim's Charter'). Other, more specialised props were put 'out to contract': Death's sword and scythe, an orangutan, the City Watch badge, a Death of Rats, a Greebo and two swamp dragons (one an elaborate hand puppet and one with a fire-proof compartment in its bottom for a flight scene).

Since the Studio Theatre Club started the trend in 1991, Terry and I have had many enquiries about staging the books – from as far afield as California, South Africa, New Zealand and Australia (as well as Sheffield, Glastonbury and the Isle of Man).

So how did our productions actually go? We enjoyed them. Our audiences seemed to enjoy them (after all, some of them were prepared, year after year, to travel down to Abingdon in Oxfordshire from as far afield as Taunton, Newcastle upon Tyne, Ipswich, Basingstoke and . . . well, Oxford). Terry seemed to enjoy them, too. He said that many of our members looked as though they had been recruited straight off the streets of Ankh-Morpork. He said that several of them were born to play the 'rude mechanicals' in Vitoller's troupe in *Wyrd Sisters*. He said that in his mind's eye the famous Ankh-Morpork City Watch *are* the players of the Studio Theatre Club.

I'm sure these were meant to be compliments.

WYRD SISTERS

We staged *Wyrd Sisters* in 1991. At the time, most of us had never heard of Terry Pratchett; his work, his readership and – above all – his audience pulling-power, were unknown factors to us. Coupled to that, we had just moved venues – from Oxford itself out to Abingdon, a small town about ten miles away.

Abingdon's mock-Elizabethan Unicorn Theatre was built, in the 1950s, in the old Abbey Buildings as a tribute to the dawn of the new Elizabethan age. The auditorium's deep-set windows, ancient walls and oak-beam ceiling were a perfect backdrop to a Shakespearian spoof set in Discworld's Lancre.

Adapting the play was more of a challenge. The first version would have run for about three hours and it was clear that a knife would have to be wielded even more mercilessly than it is in the play if we were to get down to our optimum, two-hour, running time. I had to note the main plot and to consider as optional extras any scenes that did not actually advance that main plot. I let the tax gatherer go; it was a good scene, but it mirrored the 'bun' scene. I had to let Death go! I had decided that all the other late kings of Lancre could be dispensed with without affecting the main plot and that the early scene with Verence and Death could join them; without that introduction, I could not then suddenly introduce Death into the play-within-a-play scene for his tap-dancing bit. It was a tough decision (but we made it up to HIM by staging *Mort* the following year).

The script as it appears here is now tried and tested, but it isn't the *only* way to adapt the book. Other groups have made different choices. Some have many more people available than we did, and they've looked to add in 'crowd' scenes – perhaps the late King Verence is given a bigger role and joined by Champot and his fellow spooks; Death is left in but the 'three old ladies gathering wood' is cut; the Magrat/Verence reconciliation scene is left out, and so on. Two groups entirely independently decided to add in the Standing Stone as a character. The Ankh-Morpork scenes are ripe for the knife if length becomes a problem, with the Thieves' Guild scene the first to go, particularly if your audience are not Discworld afficionados (although Monty Python fans will recognise the relentless logic of the Theft Licence). Sad, but necessary sometimes. What is important, though, is to ensure that a scene left in at one point in the play doesn't rely for part of its humour or logic on a scene you've cut elsewhere!

Inevitably, the adaptation was written with the restrictions of the Unicorn Theatre, and the numbers of players I'd have available, in mind. This meant that complicated scenic effects were virtually impossible. Anyone thinking of staging a Discworld play can be as imaginative as they like – call upon the might of Industrial Light & Magic, if it's within their budget. But they *can* be staged with fairly achievable effects, and the notes that accompany the text are intended to be a guide for those with limited or no budget.

In short, though, our experience and that of other groups is that it pays to work hard on getting the costumes and lighting right, and to keep the scenery to little more than, perhaps, a few changes of level. One group with some resourceful technophiles achieved magnificent 'scenery' simply with sound effects and lighting ('dripping water' and rippling green light for a dungeon scene, for example). There's room for all sorts of ideas here. The Discworld, as it says in the books, is your mollusc.

Characterisation
Within the constraints of what is known about and vital to each character, there is still room for flexibilty of interpretation. The witches have been played successfully with

Somerset, Dublin and Yorkshire accents (er, not in the same production!). Hwel works quite well as a Welshman, but if your right actor is the wrong height, his dwarfishness is not vital to his character. The Duke seems to work best as a twitchy version of Blackadder II, but the Duchess can be played as either an old battleaxe or, as in a couple of versions I've seen, as a more vampish wicked Queen.

The witches are each described in the Discworld canon with some detail and, if you don't wish to disappoint your audiences, it's probably an idea to try to get as close to those descriptions as you can. However, when it comes to shapes and sizes, most drama clubs don't have a vast range from which to choose and it's the acting that's more important than the look of the player when it comes to major roles!

Granny Weatherwax. In the opinion of many, not least herself, the greatest witch on the Discworld.

She is nominally the village witch of Bad Ass in the kingdom of Lancre in the Ramtops (a mountainous and unforgiving area of the Disc). For practical purposes, however, she regards the whole kingdom and, indeed, anywhere else she happens to be as her rightful domain.

She lives in the woods outside the village in a traditional, much-repaired witch's cottage, with beehives and a patch of what might be medicinal plants. She owns a broomstick, but despite the best efforts of dwarf engineers everywhere, it cannot be started without a considerable amount of running up and down with it in gear.

Esmerelda ('Granny') Weatherwax is a formidable character with every necessary attribute for the classical 'bad witch' — a quick temper, a competitive, selfish and ambitious nature, a sharp tongue, an unshakeable conviction of her own moral probity, and some considerable mental and occult powers.

Granny likes to look the part. She is tall and thin, with blue eyes and with long, fine, grey hair tied back in a severe bun. She wears sensible black, her skirt incorporates some serviceable pockets and her lace-up boots have complicated iron fixtures and toecaps like battering rams. She likes to wear several layers of clothing, including respectable flannelette petticoats. She wears a reinforced pointy hat, held in place by numerous hatpins. She has perfect skin – a source of irritation: her complexion has resisted every one of her attempts to gain some warts.

Nanny Ogg. Gytha ('Nanny') Ogg is probably in her seventies. Her family arrangements are cosy but haphazard. She has been formally married three times. All three have passed happily, if somewhat energetically, to their well-earned rest. She has fifteen living children.

Contrary to the rules of traditional witchcraft Nanny Ogg now lives in quite a modern cottage in the centre of Lancre, with up-to-date conveniences like a modern wash copper and a tin bath a mere garden's walk away on a nail at the back of the privy. The cottage is between those of her sons Shawn and Jason. She likes to have all her family around her in case of an emergency, such as when she needs a cup of tea or the floor washed.

Nanny's hair is a mass of white curls. She is a small, plump, attractive and good-natured woman, with a crinkled face, thighs that could crack coconuts and a large and experienced bosom. She smokes a pipe and, like Granny Weatherwax, she wears heavy, lace-up boots.

Magrat Garlick. A witch in Lancre. The youngest member of the coven which Granny Weatherwax swears she has not got.

Magrat has a cottage in Mad Stoat. She was selected and trained by Goodie Whemper, a methodical and sympathetic witch with a rather greater regard for the written word than is common among the Lancre witches.

In a certain light, and from a carefully chosen angle, Magrat Garlick is not unattractive. Despite her tendency to squint when she's thinking. And her pointy nose, red from too much blowing.

She is short, thin, decently plain, well-scrubbed and as flat-chested as an ironing-board with a couple of peas on it. She has the watery-eyed expression of hopeless goodwill wedged between a body like a maypole and hair like a haystack after a gale. No matter what she does to that hair, it takes about three minutes to tangle itself up again, like a garden hosepipe left in a shed. She likes to wind flowers in it, because she thinks this is romantic. She looks like someone has dropped a pot plant on her head.

Magrat has an open mind. It is as open as a field, as open as the sky. No mind could be more open without special surgical implements. A lot of what she believes in has the word 'folk' in it somewhere (folk wisdom, folk dance, folk song, folk medicine) as if 'folk' were other than the mundane people she sees every day. She thinks it would be nice if people could just be a bit kinder.

She is, however, more practical than most people believe who see no further than her vague smile, startlingly green silk dress (which would be both revealing and clinging if Magrat had anything for it to reveal or cling to) and collection of cheap occult jewellery. She is incidentally a great

xvi

believer in occult jewellery – she has three large boxes of the stuff. Although she has a black cloak lined with red silk, she hardly ever wears a pointy hat. She's just not a pointy hat person.

Costumes

Not surprisingly, we opted for coarse Shakespearian as our period, with most of the peasant characters in all-purpose combinations of tunics, tights, hoods, dresses and medieval footwear. The Duke and Duchess we attired in complementing outfits of red brocade. The late King Verence drifted around in pale grey chainmail and tunic (a bit like the knight whom Indiana Jones encounters guarding the Grail in *Indiana Jones and the Last Crusade*). Our Fool wore the traditional jester's costume, with one of those sticks with a small jester's head on the end (to which he could address the occasional remark) and a hanky with bells at each corner (which he offers to the Duke in the 'Is this a dagger I see before me?' bit).

Scenery

Well, virtually nothing. We relied on lighting changes and use of different areas and levels, together with appropriate window gobos for the castle and dungeon scenes and a green follow-spot for the late King Verence. Apart from that, just thrones for the Duke and Duchess. Stocks in the dungeon. A 'trick' entrance for the demon and so on. Stuff which is easy and quick to move on and off.

Special effects

As you'll see in the script, we had two hand-held flash devices made for us by a magic shop – one operated by clockwork, one a battery-operated flash-wool device. These were supplemented by a couple of mains-operated flash pods hired from a local firm, together with a dry ice machine; it's awful stuff to deal with, but the effect was worth it! For the flying witches we just used a follow-spot with a witch gobo plus a disco-wheel. Of these, only the flash pods are really essential.

Stephen Briggs
May 1996

TERRY PRATCHETT'S
WYRD SISTERS

adapted for the stage by Stephen Briggs

CAST OF CHARACTERS

Granny Weatherwax: *a witch*
Nanny Ogg: *a witch*
Magrat Garlick: *a witch*
Verence: *late King of Lancre*
Leonal Felmet: *Duke of Lancre*
Lady Felmet: *his wife*
Vitoller: *an actor-manager*
Mrs Vitoller: *his wife*
Fool: *a Fool*
Tomjon: *son of Verence*
Hwel: *a playwright*
Sergeant
Demon

Robbers, Players, Guests, Guards, Peasants

Play first performed by the Studio Theatre Club
at the Unicorn Theatre, Abingdon
on 15 to 18 May 1991

SCENE 1 – THE BLASTED HEATH

(The wind howls, lightning flashes and thunder crashes. A bit of dry ice would be quite nice – I know it's a swine to deal with, but it gives a good effect for the opening of the play. Around a smouldering cauldron huddle three hunched figures)

MAGRAT *(laughs maniacally)*
  When shall we three meet again? *(pause)*

GRANNY *(referring to a pocket diary)*
  Well, I can do next Tuesday.

NANNY *(referring to a diary)*
  I'm babysitting on Tuesday. For our Jason's youngest. I can manage Friday. Hurry up with the tea, luv. I'm that parched.

(Magrat sighs)

GRANNY *(patting her hand)*
  You said it quite well. Just a bit more work on the screeching. Ain't that right, Nanny Ogg?

NANNY
  Very useful screeching I thought, Granny Weatherwax. And I can see that Goody Whemper, *[NOTE – whenever Goody Whemper's name is mentioned, the three witches put their right index finger, pointing upwards, against the front*

3

of their noses, and bob (in a form of curtsey)] may-she-rest-in-peace, gave you a lot of help with the squint, Magrat.

GRANNY
It's a good squint.

MAGRAT *(flattered)*
Thank you. *(pause)* I'm glad we decided to form this coven.

NANNY
Oven?

GRANNY
Coven. Like in the old days. A meeting. *(holding up a hand)* Something comes.

MAGRAT *(earnestly)*
Can you tell by the pricking of your thumbs?

GRANNY
The pricking of my ears. *(raises her eyebrows at Nanny Ogg) (to herself)* Old Goody Whemper was an excellent witch in her own way, but far too fanciful.

NANNY
Hoofbeats? No-one would come up here this time of night.

MAGRAT *(slightly alarmed)*
What's to be afraid of?

GRANNY *(rather smugly)*
    Us.

(The hoofbeats draw nearer and halt. A soldier, enters, carry-
ing a large bundle. NOTE – he already has the crossbow
quarrel sticking out of the back of his costume, but keeps his
back away from the audience! He sees the witches and then
pauses)

GRANNY
    It's all right.

(She crosses to him. He hands her the bundle, and then topples
forward. We can now see the feathers of a crossbow bolt in his
back. Two other soldiers enter. One is carrying a crossbow. He
reaches out his hand to Granny)

BOWMAN
    You will give it to me.

GRANNY *(looks at the bundle, and then up to the Bowman)*
    No.

BOWMAN
    You are witches?

(Granny nods)

Does the skin of witches turn aside steel?

GRANNY
    Not that I'm aware. You could give it a try.

2ND SOLDIER
Sir, with respect sir, it's not a good idea—

BOWMAN
Be silent.

2ND SOLDIER
But it's terrible bad luck to—

BOWMAN
Must I ask you again?

2ND SOLDIER
Sir.

(Granny gestures; there is a flash (a flash box) to one side of the stage. [NOTE – we had Granny use a battery-powered hand-held device, bought from a magic shop, that ignited a small amount of flash wool; quite effective!] 2nd Soldier is much alarmed)

BOWMAN
Missed. Your peasant magic is for fools, mother of the night. I can strike you down where you stand.

GRANNY
Then strike, man. If your heart tells you, strike as hard as you dare.

(The man draws his sword and raises it over his head. A look of puzzlement comes over his face. He drops to his knees and falls dead to the floor. Behind him we now see the 2nd Soldier holding a blood-soaked dagger)

2ND SOLDIER
I-I-I-I couldn't let . . . He shouldn't have . . . It's not right to . . . *(a new thought)* They'll kill me now.

GRANNY
You did what you thought was right.

2ND SOLDIER
I didn't become a soldier for this. Not to go round killing people.

GRANNY
Exactly right. If I was you, I'd become a sailor. Yes, a nautical career. I should start as soon as possible.

Now, in fact. Run off, man. Run off to sea where there are no tracks. You will have a long and successful life, I promise. At least, longer than it's likely to be if you hang around here.

(He runs off)

Now, will someone please tell me what's going on?

MAGRAT
Perhaps they were bandits.

NANNY *(shaking her head)*
Strange. They both wear the same badge. Anyone know what it means?

MAGRAT
It's the badge of King Verence.

GRANNY
Who's he?

MAGRAT
He rules this country.

GRANNY *(dismissively)*
Oh. That King Verence.

NANNY *(who has opened the bundle. Gently)*
It's a baby. A baby boy. *(She rocks it gently)*

GRANNY
Anything else in there?

MAGRAT
There's this. *(She holds up a crown. It is a plain golden crown. Not jewelled, ermined or velveted)*

GRANNY
Oh. Bloody hell. First, we've got to get him out of here. A long way away, where no-one knows who he is. *(She takes the crown from Magrat)* And then there's this.

MAGRAT
Oh, that's easy. I mean, you just hide it under a stone or something. Much easier than babies.

GRANNY

It isn't. The reason being, the country's full of babies, and they all look the same. But I don't reckon there's many crowns. They have this way of being found, anyway. They kind of call out to people's minds. If you bunged it under a stone here, it'd get itself discovered by accident. You mark my words.

NANNY

It's true, that. How many time have you thrown a magic ring into the deepest depths of the ocean and then, when you get home and have a nice bit of turbot for your tea, there it is.

(They consider this)

GRANNY

Never. And nor have you. Anyway, he might want it back. If it's rightfully his, that is. Kings set a lot of store by crowns, you know. Really, Gytha, sometimes you say the most . . . what's that smell?

(They both look at the baby)

NANNY

Ah. I'll just see if there's any clean rags, eh? *(she exits)*

MAGRAT

What'd happen if we buried it somewhere?

GRANNY

The baby?

MAGRAT
The crown!

GRANNY
A badger'd dig it up. Or someone'd go prospecting for something. Or a tree'd tangle its roots around it and then get blown over in a storm, and then someone'd pick it up and put it on . . . It isn't the putting them on that's the problem. It's the taking off.

MAGRAT
It's not even as if it looked much like a crown.

GRANNY (*with sarcasm*)
You've seen a lot, I expect. You'd be an expert on them, naturally.

MAGRAT
Seen a fair few. They've got more jewels on them, and cloth bits in the middle—

GRANNY
Magrat Garlick!

MAGRAT
I have! When I was being trained by Goody Whemper . . .
(*Granny and Magrat put their fingers to their noses and bob*)

GRANNY
May–she–rest–in–peace . . .

MAGRAT *(putting her finger to her nose and bobbing)*

. . . may-she-rest-in-peace, she used to take me over to Razorback or Lancre *[NOTE – pronounced 'lanker']* whenever the strolling players were in town. She was very keen on the theatre. They've got more crowns than you could shake a stick at, although Goody used to say they're made of tin and paper and stuff. And just glass for the jewels. But they look more realler than this one. Do you think that's strange?

GRANNY

Things that try to look like things often do look more like things than things. Well-known fact. But I don't hold with encouraging it. What do they stroll around playing, then, in these crowns?

MAGRAT

Don't you know about the theatre?

GRANNY

Oh, yes. It's one of them kind of things, is it.

MAGRAT

Goody Whemper said it held a mirror up to life. She said it always cheered her up.

GRANNY

I expect it would. Played properly, at any rate. Good people, are they, these theatre players?

MAGRAT

I think so.

GRANNY
And they stroll around the country you say?

MAGRAT
All over the place. There's a troupe in Lancre now, I hear. I haven't been because, you know . . . 'tis not right, a woman going into such places by herself.

GRANNY
Right. And why not? Go and tell Gytha to wrap the baby up well. It's a long time since I heard a theatre played properly.

(Lights out)

SCENE 2 – LANCRE CASTLE

(The Duke Felmet and Lady Felmet are on stage. The Duke looks distracted, and is rubbing his hands with a grubby hanky)
[NOTE – the duke's obsession with getting his hands clean of the – imaginary – blood of King Verence can provide a good running gag that – by the play-within-a-play scene at the end of the show – can get the audience both laughing and squirming with discomfort at the same time!]

DUKE
Certainly, my dear.

DUCHESS *(The Duke's statement made no sense)*
What?

DUKE
I'll have some cut down and brought in directly, my cherished.

DUCHESS *(icily)*
Cut what down?

DUKE
Oh, the trees.

DUCHESS

What have the trees got to do with it? What I said was, how could you have been so stupid as to let them get away? I told you that servant was far too loyal. You can't trust someone like that.

DUKE

No, my love.

DUCHESS

You didn't by any chance consider sending someone after them, I suppose?

DUKE *(rather smugly)*

Bentzen, my dear, and another guard.

DUCHESS *(momentarily nonplussed by this show of competence)*

Oh. *(then)* He wouldn't have needed to go at all if only you'd listened to me. But you never do.

DUKE

Do what, my passion? *(he yawns, distractedly. He notices his hands and rubs at them, as if trying to remove a mark)*

DUCHESS

For God's sake, leave your hands alone. You've washed them five times in the last half hour.

(The Chamberlain enters)

DUKE
I can't seem to get rid of the blood. And where's the crown? I must find it.

CHAMBERLAIN
Your Majesties.

DUCHESS
And?

CHAMBERLAIN
The baby was taken by witches.

DUCHESS
Witches?

CHAMBERLAIN
Oh yes, majesty. We have them all right. Lots.

DUCHESS
And people don't do anything about them? They tolerate them?

CHAMBERLAIN
Oh, indeed. It's considered good luck to have a witch living in your village. My word, yes.

DUCHESS
Why?

CHAMBERLAIN
They smooth out life's little humps and bumps.

DUCHESS
Where I come from, they don't allow witches. And I don't propose to allow them here. You will furnish their addresses.

CHAMBERLAIN
Majesty?

DUCHESS
I trust your tax gatherers know where to find them?

(*a pause*)

DUKE
I trust that they do pay taxes?

CHAMBERLAIN
Well, not exactly pay taxes, my lord. It's more like they don't pay. The old King didn't think . . . Well, they just don't.

DUKE
I see. You may go.

(*Chamberlain exits*)

DUCHESS
Well.

DUKE
Indeed.

DUCHESS

So that was how your family used to run a kingdom, was it? You had a positive duty to kill your cousin. It was clearly in the interest of the species.

DUKE *(rubbing his hands distractedly)*

Quite so. Of course, there would appear to be many witches, and it might be difficult to find the three that were on the moor.

DUCHESS

That doesn't matter.

DUKE

Of course not.

DUCHESS

Put matters in hand.

DUKE

Yes, my petal. *(calling off)* Sergeant!

SERGEANT *(entering)*

Yes, my lord?

[NOTE – The Sergeant is a peach of a cameo. Thick, solid and literal]

DUKE

Go out into the town, and bring me a witch. In chains, if necessary.

SERGEANT *(who, despite being thick, solid and literal, can see the danger in such a course of action)*
Er...

DUKE
What?

SERGEANT *(slightly dubious, but fearful of the Duke)*
Yes, my lord. *(he salutes, and turns to exit)*

(Lights out)

SCENE 3 – THE THEATRE

(Applause. It is now after the show, and the three witches are just rising from their seats and preparing to leave)

GRANNY
Well, so that's theatre, is it? Very interesting. I wonder how they get all them kings and lords to come here and do all this. I'd have thought they'd been too busy. Ruling and similar.

MAGRAT *(wearily)*
No. I still don't think you quite understand. They're just actors, you see . . .

(One of the actors strolls past)

ACTOR
Evening.

GRANNY
You! You're dead!

(Vitoller enters. He is very much an actor-manager of the old school)

VITOLLER
May I assist you, good ladies?

GRANNY

I know you. You done the murder. Leastways, it looked like it.

VITOLLER

So glad. It is always a pleasure to meet a true connoisseur. Olwyn Vitoller, at your service. Manager of this band of vagabonds. *(He gives a low bow)*

GRANNY *(rather flattered)*
Yes, well.

NANNY

I thought you was very good, too.

MAGRAT

I hope we didn't upset things.

VITOLLER

My dear lady. Could I begin to tell you how gratifying it is for a mere mummer to learn that his audience has seen behind the mere shell of greasepaint to the spirit beneath?

GRANNY

I expect you could. I expect you could say anything, Mr Vitoller.

VITOLLER

And now, to what do I owe this visit from three such charming ladies?

20

GRANNY
We'd like to talk to you, Mr Vitoller. And Mrs Vitoller.

(Mrs Vitoller enters)

VITOLLER
Here she is. What can we do for you?

GRANNY
Mrs Vitoller, may I make so bold as to ask if your union
has been blessed with fruit?

(The couple look blank)

NANNY
She means . . .

MRS VITOLLER
No, I see. No. *(slightly ruefully – this is clearly a personal
tragedy)* We had a little girl once.

(A pause. Magrat sidles out at some stage in the following)

GRANNY
Only, you see, there is this child. And he needs a home.

VITOLLER
It is no life for a child. Always moving. Always a new
town. And no room for schooling. They say that's very
important these days.

MRS VITOLLER
Why does he need a home?

GRANNY
He hasn't got one. At least not one where he'd be welcome.

MRS VITOLLER
And you, who ask this, are by way of being his . . .?

NANNY
Godmothers.

(Vitoller and his wife look at one another. She reaches out and takes his hand. He smiles)

VITOLLER
Money is, alas, tight . . .

MRS VITOLLER
But it will stretch.

VITOLLER
Yes. I think it will. We should be happy to take care of him.

GRANNY *(taking out a purseful of coins)*
This should take care of . . . nappies and suchlike. Clothes and things. Whatever.

VITOLLER *(taken aback)*
A hundred times over, I should think. Why didn't you mention this before?

GRANNY
If I'd had to buy you, you wouldn't be worth the price.

MRS VITOLLER
But you don't know anything about us!

GRANNY *(matter-of-factly)*
We don't, do we? Naturally we'd like to hear how he gets along. You could send us letters and suchlike. But it would be a good idea not to talk about all this after you've left, do you see? For the sake of the child.

MRS VITOLLER
There's something else here, isn't there? Something big behind all this?

(Granny nods)

But it would do us no good at all to know it?

(Another nod)

VITOLLER
What's his name?

GRANNY *and* **NANNY** *(speaking simultaneously)*
Tom.   John.

GRANNY

Tom John. We'll come back, with the boy.

(Vitoller bows. He and Mrs Vitoller exit) (Magrat re-enters)

MAGRAT

I found a box. It had all the crowns and things in. So I put it in, like you said, right underneath everything.

GRANNY

Good.

MAGRAT

Our crown looked really tatty compared to the others.

GRANNY

Did anyone see you?

MAGRAT

No, everyone was too busy . . . but—

GRANNY

Yes?

MAGRAT *(very naive)*

Just after I'd hidden it a man came up and . . . pinched my bottom.

GRANNY

And?

MAGRAT
And then . . . and then . . . he said . . .

NANNY
What did he say?

MAGRAT
He said, 'Hello, my lovely, what are you doing tonight?'

GRANNY *(after a pause)*
Old Goody Whemper, she didn't get out and about much, did she?

MAGRAT
It was her leg, you know.

NANNY
But she taught you midwifery and everything?

MAGRAT
Oh, yes, that. I done lots.

GRANNY
But . . . she never talked to you about what you might call the previous.

MAGRAT
Sorry?

GRANNY
You know . . . men and such.

MAGRAT
What about them?

GRANNY *(giving up the challenge)*
I think that it might be a good idea if you have a quiet word with Nanny Ogg one of these days. *(with a look at Nanny)* Fairly soon.

(Lights out)

SCENE 4 – THE CASTLE

(The Sergeant is on stage, at attention. The Duke is also on stage. At the rear of the stage, the Fool sits) [NOTE – this scene is a gift to those involved; think of Rowan Atkinson's Blackadder II as the Duke and Tony Robinson's Baldrick (or Hugh Laurie's Prince Regent) as the Sergeant]

DUKE
  She did what?

SERGEANT
  She give me a cup of tea, sir.

DUKE
  And what about your men?

SERGEANT
  She give them one, too, sir.

DUKE *(putting his arm round the Sergeant's shoulder)*
  Sergeant.

SERGEANT
  Sir?

DUKE *(charming, but threatening)*

I mean, it is possible I may have confused you. I meant to say 'Bring me a witch, in chains, if necessary', but perhaps what I really said was 'Go and have a cup of tea'. Was this in fact the case?

SERGEANT *(unused to sarcasm)*

No, sir.

DUKE

I wonder why, then, you did not in fact do this thing that I asked?

SERGEANT

Sir?

DUKE

I expect she said some magic words, did she? I've heard about witches. I imagine she offered you visions of unearthly delight? Did she show you . . . *(he shudders as some sordid thought passes through his mind)* . . . dark fascinations and forbidden raptures, the like of which mortal men should not even think of, and demonic secrets that took you to the depths of man's desires? *(sits down and fans himself with a handkerchief)*

SERGEANT

Are you all right, sir?

DUKE

What? Oh, perfectly, perfectly.

SERGEANT
Only you've gone all red.

DUKE *(snapping)*
Don't change the subject, man. Admit it – she offered you hedonistic and licentious pleasures known only to those who dabble in the carnal arts, didn't she?

SERGEANT
No, sir. She offered me a bun.

(Pause)

DUKE
A bun?

SERGEANT
Yes, sir. It had currants in it.

DUKE *(with great restraint)*
And what did your men do about this?

SERGEANT
They had a bun, too, sir. All except young Roger, who isn't allowed fruit, sir, on account of his trouble.

(A pause as the Duke looks at him, knowing he will tell him what Roger had)

He had a biscuit, sir.

(The Duke struggles to keep control. This brings on his paranoia about his hands. He rubs them distractedly)

DUKE
You may go, Sergeant.

SERGEANT
Sir.

(He marches out)

DUKE
Fool?

FOOL *(capering to him and striking a pose. Nervously)*
Marry, sir . . .

DUKE
I am already extremely married. Advise me, my Fool.

FOOL
I'faith, nuncle . . .

DUKE
Nor am I thy nuncle. I feel sure I would have remembered. *(he leans forward until his face is very close to the Fool's)* If you preface your next remark with nuncle, i'faith or marry, it will go hard with you.

FOOL *(after a moment's thought)*
How do you feel about 'prithee'?

DUKE

Prithee I can live with. *(meaningful pause)* So can you. But no capering. *(with an encouraging grin)* How long have you been a Fool, boy?

FOOL

Prithee, sirrah—

DUKE

The sirrah . . . on the whole, I think not.

FOOL

Prithee, sirra. . . . sir. All my life, sir. Seventeen years under the bladder, man and boy. And my father before me. And my nuncle at the same time as him. And my granddad before them. And his—

DUKE

Your whole family have been Fools?

FOOL

Family tradition, sir.

DUKE

You come from these parts, don't you?

FOOL

Ma— Yes, sir.

DUKE

So you would know about the native beliefs and so on?

FOOL
I suppose so, sir. Prithee.

DUKE
Good. Tell me about witches.

(The Duchess enters)

DUCHESS
But not now. Well, where are the witches?

DUKE
The Chamberlain would appear to be right, beloved.
The witches seem to have the local people in thrall. The
sergeant of the guard came back empty-handed. *(to
himself; the word has struck a chord)* Handed . . . handed.

DUCHESS
You must have him executed. To make an example to
the others.

DUKE
A course of action, my dear, which ultimately results in
us ordering the last soldier to cut his own throat as an
example to himself. By the way, there seem to be fewer
servants around than usual.

DUCHESS
Housekeeping is under my control. I cannot abide slack-
ness! What of these witches? Will you stand idly by and
let trouble seed for the future? Will you let these witches
defy you? What of the crown?

DUKE *(with a shrug)*
No doubt it ended in the river.

DUCHESS
And the child? He was given to the witches. Do they do human sacrifice?

DUKE *(with a disappointed air)*
Apparently not. These witches . . . apparently they seem to cast a spell on people.

DUCHESS
Well, obviously—

DUKE
Not like a magic spell. They seem to be respected. They do medicine and so on. It might be difficult to move against them.

DUCHESS
I could come to believe that they have cast a glamour over you as well. In fact, you like it, don't you? The thought of the danger. I remember when we were married; all that business with that knotted rope—

DUKE *(snapping)*
Not at all!

DUCHESS
Then what will you do?

DUKE
Wait.

DUCHESS
Wait?

DUKE
Wait and consider. Patience is a virtue.

(He starts to rub absent-mindedly at his hands. The Duchess leans over and slaps his wrist as the lights black out)

SCENE 5 – WITCH'S COTTAGE

(Magrat and Nanny are on stage. Granny enters)

GRANNY
Good evening.

MAGRAT
Well met by moonlight. Merry meet. A star shines on —

NANNY
Wotcha.

GRANNY *(with a wince)*
Anyway, how goes it, sisters?

MAGRAT
If we're going to start, we'd better light the candles.

(Nanny and Granny exchange looks)

GRANNY
Candle.

NANNY
And a decent white one. Nothing fancy. *(they sit. Magrat lights the candle)* What about this new duke, then?

GRANNY
He had some houses burned down in Bad Ass. Because of the taxes.

MAGRAT
How horrible.

NANNY
Old King Verence used to do that. Terrible temper he had.

GRANNY
He used to let people out first though.

NANNY
Oh, yes, he could be very gracious like that. He'd pay for them to be rehoused as often as not. If he remembered. And then there was that great hairy thing of his.

GRANNY
Ah, yes. His 'droit de seigneur'.

NANNY
Needed a lot of exercise.

GRANNY
But next day he'd send his housekeeper with a bag of silver and a hamper of stuff for the wedding. Many a couple got a proper start in life thanks to that.

MAGRAT
What are you two talking about? Did he keep pets?

(The other two exchange glances and shrug)

Did you know that no-one is allowed to say that Felmet killed the king? He had some people executed in Lancre the other day. Spreading malicious lies, he said. He said Verence died of natural causes.

GRANNY
Well, being assassinated is natural causes for a king. I think we have to keep an eye on this one. I think he might be a bit clever. That's not a good thing, in a king. And he don't know how to show respect.

MAGRAT
A man came to see me last week to ask if I wanted to pay any taxes. I told him no.

NANNY
He came to see me, too. But our Jason and our Wayne went out and told him we didn't want to join.

GRANNY
Small man, black cloak?

NANNY *and* **MAGRAT**
Yes.

GRANNY

He was hanging around in my raspberry bushes. Only, when I went out to see what he wanted, he ran away.

(Pause. Magrat looks a bit embarrassed)

MAGRAT

Actually, I gave him tuppence.

(The other two 'tut' and sigh)

He was going to be tortured, you see, if he didn't get the witches to pay their taxes.

(Granny and Nanny exchange glances as the lights black out)

SCENE 6 – THE CASTLE

(The Duke and the Fool are on stage. The Duke is now using sand-paper on his hands, which are beginning to show signs of this abuse, looking a bit raw)

DUKE
Tell me, Fool, does it always rain here?

FOOL
Marry, nuncle —

DUKE *(with iron patience)*
Just answer the question.

FOOL
Sometimes it stops, sir. To make room for the snow. And sometimes we get some right squand'ring orgulous fogs.

DUKE
Orgulous?

FOOL
Thick, my lord. From the Latatian 'orgulum', a soup or broth.

DUKE

I am bored, Fool.

FOOL

Let me entertain you, my lord, with many a merry quip and lightsome jest.

DUKE

Try me.

(A pause)

I'm waiting. Make me laugh.

FOOL *(taking the plunge)*

Why, sirrah, why may a caudled fillhorse be deemed the brother to a hiren candle in the night?

(The Duke frowns)

Withal, because a candle may be greased, yet a fillhorse be without fat argier. *(he pats the Duke lightly with the balloon)*

DUKE *(after a deadpan pause)*

Yes. And then what happened?

FOOL

That, er, was by way of being the whole thing. My granddad thought it was one of his best.

DUKE
I dare say he told it differently.

(There is a sudden rumbling, as of an earthquake. The Duke and the Fool stagger somewhat — a bit like 'Voyage to the Bottom of the Sea')

What's happening? Is it an earthquake?

FOOL
We don't have them in these parts, my lord.

DUKE
It's the witches, isn't it? They're out to get me, aren't they?

FOOL
Marry, nuncle—

DUKE
They run this country, don't they?

FOOL
No, my lord, they never—

DUKE
Who asked you?

FOOL
Er, you did, my lord.

DUKE

Are you arguing with me?

FOOL

No, my lord!

DUKE

I thought so. You're in league with them, I suppose.

FOOL

My lord!

DUKE

You're all in league, you people! I am the king! Do you all hear me? I am the king!

(He starts to sniffle. The Fool crosses to him and holds out his hanky to him – it matches his costume and has little bells sown on the corners. The Duke doesn't see it)

Is this a dagger I see before me?

FOOL

Um. No, my lord. It's my handkerchief, you see. You can sort of tell the difference if you look closely. It doesn't have as many sharp edges.

DUKE

Good Fool. Are you loyal, Fool? Are you trustworthy?

FOOL

I swore to follow my lord until death.

42

(The Duke leans towards him, conspiratorially)

DUKE
I didn't want to. They made me do it. I didn't—

DUCHESS *(entering)*
Leonal!

DUKE
Yes, my dear?

DUCHESS
What was that earthquake?

DUKE
Witches, I suspect.

DUCHESS
So. They still defy you?

DUKE
How should I fight magic?

FOOL
With words.

DUCHESS
What?

FOOL *(nervous)*
In . . . in the Guild, we learned that words can be more powerful even than magic.

43

DUKE

Clown! Words are just words. Brief syllables. Sticks and stones may break my bones, but words can never hurt me.

FOOL

My lord, there are such words that can. Liar! Usurper! Murderer! *(he adds, quickly)* Such words have no truth. But they can spread like fire underground, breaking out to burn—

DUKE

It's true! It's true! I hear them all the time! *(hissing)* It's the witches!

FOOL

Then, then, then they can be fought with other words. Words can fight even witches . . .

DUCHESS *(thoughtfully)*

What words?

FOOL *(with a shrug)*

Crone. Evil eye. Stupid old woman.

DUCHESS

You are not entirely an idiot, are you? You refer to rumour.

FOOL

Just so, my lady.

DUKE *(to no-one in particular)*
It's the witches. We must tell the world about the witches. They're evil. They make it come back, the blood. *(he rubs at his hands)* Even sandpaper doesn't work.

(Duke and Duchess exit as he speaks. The Fool is left alone, to soliloquise)

FOOL *(speaking to his Jester's stick)*
What have I got myself into? I never asked to be a Fool, you know. It just happened. First thing I can remember is Granddad standing over me, making me repeat the jokes by rote, hammering home every punchline with his belt.

He was credited with seven official new jokes, you know. He won the honorary cap and bells of the Grand Prix des Idiots at Ankh-Morpork three years in a row.

I remember, when I was about seven, I tried to make up a joke. When I told Granddad he gave me the biggest thrashing of my life: 'You will learn, lad, that there is nothing more serious than jesting.' *(miming the thrashing)*

Never, never, ever, utter a joke that has not been approved by the Guild. Never, never, never let me catch you *joculating* again. *(he sighs, and exits as . . . lights out)*

SCENE 7 – WITCH'S HOUSE

(Nanny is on stage. Granny and Magrat enter)

NANNY

What ho, me old boiler. See you turned up then. Have a
drink. Have two. Watcher, Magrat. Pull up a chair and
call the cat a bastard. Actually, don't think you can.

MAGRAT

Can what?

NANNY

Call the cat a bastard. He's disappeared, old Greebo.
Haven't seen him for a couple of days. *(a new thought)*
Here, what about that earthquake, then?

GRANNY

Extremely worrying developments of a magical tendency are even now afoot.

NANNY

Well, we'd better have a look, then. *(she takes the lid off
her wash copper)* I think perhaps we should join hands.
Is the door shut?

(Magrat nods)

GRANNY

What are you going to try?

46

NANNY
I always say you can't go wrong with a good Invocation. Haven't done one for years.

MAGRAT
Oh, but you can't. Not here. You need a cauldron, and a magic sword. And an octogram. And spices, all sorts of stuff.

(Nanny and Granny exchange glances)

GRANNY
It's not her fault. It's all them grimmers she bought.

MAGRAT
Grimoires.

GRANNY
You don't need none of that. You just use whatever you've got. *(she picks up a rolling pin, holds it aloft and declaims)* We conjure and abjure thee by means of this . . . weighty and terrible rolling pin.

MAGRAT *(picking up a packet of soap flakes)*
See how we scatter *(she sighs)* rather old washing soda and some extremely hard soap flakes in thy honour. Really, Nanny, I don't think—

NANNY
And I invoke and bind thee with the balding scrubbing brush of Art and the washboard of Protection.

MAGRAT
Honesty is all very well, but somehow it just isn't the same.

GRANNY
You listen to me, girl. Demons don't care about the outward shape of things. It's what you think that matters. Get on with it.

(They all look, in deepest concentration, at the copper. Smoke rises from it, and a head appears) *[NOTE – we couldn't do the copper, so we had our demon appear out of a, very shallow, drawer apparently full of laundry, placed over an unseen trapdoor in the Unicorn's stage]*

DEMON
Well?

GRANNY
Who're you?

DEMON
My name is unpronounceable in your tongue, woman.

GRANNY
I'll be the judge of that. And don't you call me woman.

DEMON
Very well. My name is WxrtHlt-jwlpklz.

48

NANNY

Where were you when the vowels were handed out? Behind the door?

GRANNY

Well, Mr . . . WxrtHlt–jwlpklz *(it's a good effort, and pretty close to the Demon's pronunciation)*, I expect you're wondering why we called you here tonight.

DEMON

You're not supposed to say that. You're supposed to say—

GRANNY

Shut up. We have the sword of Art and the octogram of Protection, I warn you.

DEMON

They look like a balding scrubbing brush and a washboard to me. You are allowed three questions.

GRANNY *(to the others)*

We must be careful; Demons always tell the truth, but only as much as they need to. We must phrase our questions very carefully. *(to the Demon)* Is there something strange at large in the kingdom?

DEMON

You mean stranger than usual? No. There is nothing strange.

GRANNY
Hold on, hold on. *(she tries again)* Is there something in the kingdom that wasn't there before?

DEMON
No.

GRANNY *(a last try)*
What the hell's going on? And no mucking about trying to wriggle out of it, otherwise I'll boil you.

(The Demon hesitates at this new approach)

Magrat, just bring over that kindling, will you?

DEMON
I protest at this treatment.

GRANNY
Yes, well. I haven't got time to bandy legs with you all night. These word games might be all very well for wizards, but we've other fish to fry.

NANNY
Or boil.

DEMON *(a little worried now)*
Look, we're not supposed to volunteer information just like that. There are rules, you know.

NANNY
There's some old oil in the can in the shed, Magrat.

DEMON

If I simply tell you . . .

GRANNY *(encouragingly)*

Yes?

DEMON

You won't let on, will you?

GRANNY

Not a word.

MAGRAT

Lips are sealed.

DEMON

There is nothing new in the Kingdom, but the land has woken up.

GRANNY

What do you mean?

DEMON

It's unhappy. It wants a king that cares for it.

GRANNY

You don't mean the people, do you?

(Demon shakes its head)

No, I didn't think so.

NANNY
   What —?

(Granny holds up a hand)

GRANNY
   Can you tell us why?

DEMON
   I'm just a demon. What do I know? Only what it is, not
   the why and how of it.

GRANNY
   I see.

DEMON
   May I go now?

GRANNY
   Mmm?

DEMON
   Please?

GRANNY
   Oh. Yes. Run along. Thank you.

DEMON *(after a pause)*
   You wouldn't mind banishing me, would you?

GRANNY *(still distracted)*
What?

DEMON

Only I'd feel better if I was properly banished. 'Run along' lacks that certain something.

GRANNY

Oh, well. If it gives you pleasure. Magrat! Do the honours, will you?

MAGRAT

Certainly. Right. Okay. Um. Begone, foul fiend, unto the blackest pit . . .

(The head starts to sink back into the copper. As it goes . . .)

DEMON

Run aaaalonggg . . .

NANNY

Well. I wonder if that's why Greebo's vanished.

GRANNY

Cats can look after themselves. Countries can't. Duke Felmet hates the kingdom. The villagers say that when they go to see him he just stares at them and giggles and rubs his hands and twitches.

NANNY

The old king used to shout at them and kick them out of the castle. But he was always very gracious about it. You felt he meant it. People like to feel they're valued.

GRANNY

The kingdom is worried. You heard what the demon said. This morning when I opened my door, there were all the animals of the forest, just stood outside.

MAGRAT

What did they say?

GRANNY

Nothing. Animals, aren't they? Knew what they wanted, though. Rid of the king. They was sent, by the kingdom, the land itself. It doesn't care if people are good or bad. But it expects the king to care for it.

MAGRAT

It's a bit like a dog, really. A dog doesn't care if its master's good or bad, just so long as it likes the dog.

NANNY

What are we going to do about it?

GRANNY

Nothing. You know we can't meddle.

NANNY

You saved the baby.

GRANNY

That's not meddling!

NANNY
Have it your way. But maybe one day he'll come back. Destiny again.

GRANNY
Right.

(Pause)

MAGRAT
You know the Fool, who lives up at the castle?

NANNY
Little man with runny eyes?

MAGRAT
Not that little. What's his name, do you happen to know?

GRANNY
He's just called Fool. No job for a man, that. Running around with bells on.

NANNY
His mother was a Beldame, from over Blackglass way. Bit of a beauty when she was younger. Broke many a heart, she did. Bit of a scandal there, I did hear. Think he was named after his master the king. Verence. Granny's right, though. At the end of the day, a Fool's a Fool.

GRANNY

Why d'you want to know, Magrat?

MAGRAT *(blushing)*

Oh . . . one of the girls in the village was asking me.

(Nanny clears her throat, and nudges Granny)

NANNY

It's a steady job. I'll grant you that.

GRANNY

Huh. A man who tinkles all day. No kind of a husband
for anyone, I'd say.

NANNY

You . . . she'd always know where he was. You'd just
have to listen.

GRANNY

Never trust a man with horns on his hat.

MAGRAT *(suddenly)*

You're a pair of silly old women. And I'm going home!
(she stalks out)

GRANNY *and* NANNY

Well!

(Lights out)

SCENE 8 – THE CASTLE DUNGEON

(*Noise of echoey dripping water. Nanny, the Duke and Duchess are on stage. Also on stage is King Verence (in a green follow-spot), sitting in a corner and watching the action. Nanny is in the stocks. The Duke's hands are now a bit bloody, and he is working away at them using a rather rusty-looking rasp*)

DUKE

Quite comfortable, are we?

NANNY

Apart from these stocks, you mean?

DUKE

I am impervious to your foul blandishments. I scorn your devious wiles. You are to be tortured, I'll have you know.

DUCHESS (*since that seems to have had no effect*)

And then you will be burned.

NANNY

Okay.

DUKE

Okay?

NANNY

Well, it's bloody freezing down here. What's that big wardrobe thing with the spikes?

DUKE

Aha. Now you realise, do you? That, my dear lady, is the Iron Maiden. It's the latest thing. Well may you . . .

NANNY

Can I have a go in it?

DUKE

Your pleas fall on deaf . . .what?

DUCHESS

This insouciance gives you pleasure, but soon you'll laugh on the other side of your face!

NANNY

It's only got this side.

DUCHESS *(fingering a pair of pliers)*

We shall see.

DUKE

And you need not think any others of your people will come to your aid. We alone hold the keys of this dungeon. Ha ha. You will be an example to all those who have been spreading malicious rumours about me. I hear the voices all the time, lying . . .

DUCHESS

Enough! Come, Leonal. We will let her reflect on her fate for a while.

DUKE *(muttering, as he exits)*

... the faces ... wicked lies ... I wasn't there, and anyway he fell ...

(A moment's silence)

NANNY

All right. I can see you. Who are you?

(King Verence steps forward)

I saw you making faces behind him. All I could do to keep a straight face.

VERENCE

I wasn't making faces, woman. I was scowling.

NANNY

'Ere, I know you. You're dead. You're the late King Verence.

VERENCE

I prefer the term 'passed over'. I'm afraid it was I who borrowed your cat: I knew you'd come looking for it.

NANNY

What's that big bed thing over there?

VERENCE
The rack.

NANNY
Oh. I suppose you're no good at locks?

VERENCE *(shaking his head)*
But surely, to a witch this is all so much . . .

NANNY
Solid iron. You might be able to walk through it, but I can't.

VERENCE
I didn't realise. I thought witches could do magic.

NANNY
Young man, you will oblige me by shutting up!

VERENCE
Madam! I am a king!

NANNY
You are also dead, so I wouldn't aspire to hold any opinions if I was you.

(Pause. Lights go down and up to indicate the passage of time. During the brief blackout a clock chimes)

I spy, with my little eye, something beginning with P.

VERENCE
Oh. Er, Pliers.

NANNY
  No.

VERENCE
  Pilliwinks?

NANNY
  That's a pretty name. What's that?

VERENCE
  It's a kind of thumbscrew.

NANNY
  No.

VERENCE
  Choke-pear?

NANNY
  That's a C, and anyway I don't know what it is. You're
  a bit too good at these names. You sure you didn't use
  them when you were alive?

VERENCE
  Absolutely, Nanny.

NANNY
  Boys that tell lies go to a bad place.

VERENCE
  Lady Felmet had most of them installed herself. It's the
  truth.

NANNY
All right. It was 'pinchers'.

VERENCE
But that's just another name for pliers. (*pause*) They'll
be back soon. Are you sure you'll be all right?

NANNY
If I'm not, how much help can you be?

(*A sound of bolts sliding back. The Duke, Duchess and Fool
enter*)

DUCHESS
We will begin with the Showing of the Implements.

NANNY
Seen 'em. Leastways all the ones beginning with P, S, I,
T and W.

DUCHESS
Then let us see how long you can keep that light conver-
sational tone.

NANNY
Is this going to take long? I haven't had breakfast.

DUCHESS
Now, woman, will you confess?

NANNY
What to?

DUCHESS
It's common knowledge. Treason. Malicious witchcraft. Harbouring the king's enemies. Theft of the crown and spreading false rumours.

NANNY
What false rumours?

DUKE *(hoarsely)*
Concerning the accidental death of the late King Verence.

NANNY
Oh, I don't know nothing false.

(Verence whispers to her, telling her what happened)

I know you stabbed him, and you gave him the dagger. It was at the top of the stairs. Just by the suit of armour with the pike. And you said, 'If it's to be done, it's better if it's done quickly' or something, and then you snatched the king's own dagger . . .

DUKE
You lie! There were no witnesses. We made . . . there was nothing to witness! I heard someone in the dark, but there was no-one there!

DUCHESS
Do shut up, Leonal!

DUKE

Who told her? Did you tell her?

DUCHESS

And calm down. No-one told her. She's a witch, for goodness sake, they find out about these things. Second glance, or something.

NANNY

Sight.

DUCHESS

Which you will not possess much longer, my good woman, unless you tell us who else knows and indeed assist us on a number of other matters. (*pause*) And now we will commence. Your friends can't help you now.

(Lights out)

SCENE 9 – CASTLE GATEHOUSE

(Guards and crowd on stage. Granny enters, carrying a basket of apples)

PEASANT *(to Granny)*
There's a witch in the dungeons. And foul tortures, they say.

GRANNY
Nonsense. I expect Nanny Ogg has just gone in to advise the king, or something.

PEASANT
They say Jason Ogg's gone to fetch his brothers.

GRANNY
I really advise you all to return home. There has probably been a misunderstanding. Everyone knows a witch cannot be held against her will.

PEASANT
It's gone too far this time. All this burning and taxing and now this. I blame you witches. It's got to stop. I know my rights.

GRANNY
And what rights are they?

PEASANT

Dunnage, cowage-in-ordinary, badinage, leftovers, scrommidge, clary and spunt. And acornage every other year. And the right to keep two-thirds of a goat on the common. Until he set fire to it. *(pause)* It was a bloody good goat, too.

GRANNY

A man could go far, knowing his rights like you do. *(a hint of threat)* But right now he should go home.

(The peasants exit. Granny turns and looks at the guards)

I am a harmless old seller of apples. Pray let me past, dearie.

GUARD 1

No-one must enter the castle. Orders of the Duke.

GRANNY

I know you, Champett Poldy. I recall I laid out your granddad and I brought you into the world. *(leaning in to him)* I gave you your first good hiding in this vale of tears and by all the gods if you cross me now I will give you your last. *(He drops his spear. Granny pats his shoulder)* But don't worry about it. Have an apple.

GUARD 2

So that's witches' magic, is it? Pretty poor stuff. Maybe it frightens these country idiots, woman, but it doesn't frighten me.

GRANNY

I imagine it takes a lot to frighten a big, strong lad like you.

GUARD 2

And don't you try to put the wind up me, neither. Old ladies like you, twisting people around. It shouldn't be stood for, like they say.

GRANNY *(pushing his spear aside)*

Just as you like . . .

GUARD 2 *(grabbing her)*

Listen, I said . . . *(suddenly, he is clutching at his arm and moaning)*

(Granny puts her hatpin back in her hat and exits, triumphant. Almost before the guards have rearranged themselves, Magrat enters, also bearing a basket of apples)

GUARD 1

Oh my God.

MAGRAT

I've come to sell my lovely apples.

GUARD 2

There's not a sale on, is there? *(it dawns on him)* You're not a witch, are you?

MAGRAT

Of course not. Do I look like one?

GUARD 2 *(uncertainly)*
Right. *(He looks at her. Pointed hat, black cloak, etc.)*
Pass, apple seller.

MAGRAT
Thank you. Would you like an apple?

GUARD 1
No, thanks. I haven't finished the one the other witch gave me. Not a witch. Apple seller.

MAGRAT
How long ago was this?

GUARD 1
Just a few minutes . . .

(Magrat exits quickly)

An apple seller. Yes. Well, she should know.

(Lights out)

SCENE 10 – OUTSIDE THE DUNGEON

(A corridor in the castle. Two guards on stage. Magrat enters)

GUARD 3
Well, well. Come to keep us company, have you, my pretty?

MAGRAT
I was looking for the dungeons.

GUARD 3
Just fancy. I reckon we can help you there. *(he puts an arm around her waist)*

MAGRAT
I think I should warn you. I am not, as I may appear, a simple apple seller. *(no reaction)* I am in fact a witch.

GUARD 3
Fair enough. I've always wondered what it was like to kiss a witch. Around here they do say you gets turned into a frog.

GUARD 4 *(nudging him)*
I reckon, then, you kissed one years ago. *(he laughs)*

(Guards shove Magrat up against the wall)

GUARD 3

Now listen to me, sweetheart. You ain't the first witch we've had down here, but you could be lucky, and walk out of here. If you're nice to us, that is. *(he mauls her a bit)* Here, what's this? A knife? I reckon we've got to take this very seriously, don't you, Hron?

GUARD 4

You got to tie her hands and gag her. They can't do magic if they can't speak or wave their hands about . . .

FOOL *(who has entered suddenly)*

You can take your hands off her! Let her go this minute! Or I'll report you!

GUARD 3

This is a witch we have here. So you can go and tinkle somewhere else. *(he turns back to Magrat)* I like a girl with spirit.

FOOL

I told you to let her go.

(Guard 4 draws his sword. Suddenly Magrat lashes out at Guard 3 with all her might. He spins around with the force of the blow and crashes to the floor. Guard 4 turns in amazement to see his colleague laid out. The Fool charges at him, knocking him over. He grabs the Fool around the throat, but Magrat comes up behind him and holds a knife to his throat)

MAGRAT
Let go of him. *(a pause)* You're wondering whether I really would cut your throat. I don't know either. Think of the fun we could have together, finding out.

(Both guards get to their feet)

Right. And now. Run away.

(They exit)

(To Fool) Right, now where is she?

FOOL *(crossing to the door)*
It's locked.

MAGRAT
Well, it's a dungeon, isn't it?

FOOL
They're not supposed to lock it from the inside.

(Magrat examines the door)

Are you really a witch? You don't look like one. You look very . . . that is . . . not like a, you know, crone at all, but absolutely beautiful . . .

MAGRAT *(a little flustered by this)*
I think you'd better stand back, Verence. I'm not sure how this is going to work.

FOOL
How did you know my name?

MAGRAT *(examining the door)*
Oh, I expect I heard it somewhere.

FOOL
I shouldn't think so, I never use it. I mean, it's not a popular name with the Duke. It was me mam, you see. They like to name you after kings, I suppose...

(Magrat holds up her hand. There is a small flash) [We used a handheld clockwork device, bought from a magic shop, that 'fires' sparks through the fingers]

Is that it?

MAGRAT
Wait. It's not over yet.

(Granny enters)

GRANNY
Good technique. But it's all old wood. Lot of iron nails and stuff in there. Can't see it working...

(There is an almighty flash, and an explosion (sound effect))

(Lights out)

SCENE 11 – THE CASTLE DUNGEON

[We repeated the flash, to give the effect that 'we' are now see-ing the events in the corridor from inside the cell.] *(Nanny, Duke and Duchess (with Verence) are inside. Granny, Magrat and Fool enter. Magrat and the Fool stay to one side of the stage)*

NANNY
Took your time. Let me out of this, will you? I'm getting cramp.

VERENCE
My own dagger! All this time and I never knew it! They bloody well did me in with my own bloody knife!

GRANNY
Isn't that the old king? Can they see him?

NANNY
Shouldn't think so.

DUCHESS
Guards! Fool, fetch the guards!

GRANNY
They're busy. We were just leaving. Are you the duke?

(The Duke nods)

I'm going to give you no cause. But it would be better for you if you left this country. Abdicate, or whatever.

DUCHESS
In favour of whom? A witch?

DUKE
I won't.

GRANNY
What did you say?

DUKE
I said I won't. Do you think a bit of simple conjuring would frighten me? I am king by right of conquest and you cannot change it. It is as simple as that, witch. *(a pause as he lets this sink in)* If you defeat me by magic, magic will rule. You can't do it. Any king raised with your help would be under your power. Hag-ridden, I might say. That which magic rules, it destroys. It would destroy you, too. You know it. Ha, ha.

(Granny's knuckles whiten)

You *could* strike me down, and perhaps you could replace me. But he would have to be fool indeed, because he would know he was under your evil eye, and if he displeased you, why, his life would be instantly forfeit. You could protest all you wished, but he'd know he ruled with your permission. And that would make him no king at all. Is not that true? *(a pause)* I said, is that not true?

GRANNY

Yes. Yes, it is true . . . but there is one who could defeat you.

DUKE *(sneering)*

The child? Let him come when he is grown. A young man with a sword, to seek his destiny. Very romantic. But I have many years to prepare. Let him try. *(nose to nose with Granny, he hisses)* Get back to your cauldrons, wyrd sisters.

(The Duke turns on his heel, and swoops out. Rather taken aback, the Duchess follows. Offstage, we hear the Duke laughing)

NANNY

You could give him boils or something. Haemorrhoids are good. That's allowed. It won't stop him ruling, it just means he'll have to rule standing up. Always good for a laugh that. *(pause)* Mind you, that'd probably make him worse. Same with toothache.

GRANNY

I ain't going to give him the pleasure of saying it, but he's got us beaten.

NANNY

Well, I don't know. Our Jason and a few lads could soon . . .

GRANNY

You saw some of his guards. These aren't the old sort. These are a tough kind.

NANNY

We could give the boys a bit of help.

GRANNY

It wouldn't work. People have to sort this sort of thing out for themselves. Magic's there to be ruled, not to do the ruling.

FOOL *(who has been plucking up his courage)*

Can I see you again?

MAGRAT

Oh no. I'm very busy tonight.

FOOL

Tomorrow night, then?

MAGRAT

I think I should be washing my hair.

FOOL

I could get Friday night free.

MAGRAT
We do a lot of work at night, see . . .

FOOL
The afternoon, then?

MAGRAT
Well . . .

FOOL
About two o'clock. In the meadow by the pond, all right?

MAGRAT
Well . . .

FOOL
See you there, then. All right?

DUCHESS (*off*)
Fool!

FOOL
I've got to go. The meadow, Okay? I'll wear a flower so
you recognise me. All right?

MAGRAT
All right.

(Fool exits)

NANNY
Esme, there's someone here to see you.

VERENCE
Verence, king of Lancre. Do I have the honour of addressing Granny Weatherwax, doyenne of witches?

(Granny nods, modestly)

I beg you, Granny Weatherwax, to restore my son to the throne.

GRANNY
It's meddling, you see.

VERENCE
You're not going to help?

GRANNY
Well . . . naturally, one day, when your lad is a bit older . . .

VERENCE (*coldly*)
Where is he now?

GRANNY
We saw him safe out of the country, you see.

NANNY
Very good family.

VERENCE
What kind of people? Not commoners, I trust?

GRANNY
Absolutely not. Not common at all. Very uncommon.
Erm . . .

MAGRAT
They were Thespians.

VERENCE
Oh. Good.

NANNY
Were they? They didn't look it.

GRANNY
Don't show your ignorance, Gytha Ogg. Sorry about
that, Your Majesty. It's just her showing off. She don't
even know where Thespia is.

VERENCE
Wherever it is, I hope they know how to school a man in
the arts of war. I know Felmet. In ten years he'll be dug
in like a toad in a stone. What kind of kingdom will he
come back to? Will you watch it change, over the years,
become shoddy and mean? *(he starts to drift out)*
Remember, good sisters, the land and the king are one.

(And he has gone)

NANNY
One what?

GRANNY

We've got to do something. Rules or no rules! Lock up a witch, would he? I'll bloody well show him what a witch can do!

NANNY

Yes, yes, only perhaps not right now. Let's plan—

GRANNY

Wyrd sisters indeed! We'll meet on the heath tonight and decide what must be done! *(She strides out)*

MAGRAT

Whatever happened to the rule about not meddling in politics?

NANNY

Ah. The thing is, as you progress in the Craft, you'll learn there is another rule. Esme's obeyed it all her life.

MAGRAT

And what's that?

NANNY

When you break rules, break 'em good and hard!

(Lights out)

SCENE 12 – THE CASTLE

(Duke, Duchess and Fool are on stage. The Duke is now working away at his, very bloody, hands with a rusty cheesegrater)

DUKE
It works. The people mutter against the witches. How do you do it, Fool?

FOOL
Jokes, nuncle. And gossip. People are halfway ready to believe it anyway. Everyone respects the witches. The point is that no-one actually likes them very much.

DUKE
This is very pleasing. If it goes on like this, Fool, you shall have a knighthood.

FOOL
Marry, nuncle, if 'n I had a Knighthood – Night Hood – why, it would keep my ears warm in Bedde; i'Faith, if many a Knight is a Fool, why then . . .

DUKE
Yes, yes, all right.

DUCHESS
It seems that words are extremely powerful.

FOOL
Indeed, lady.

DUCHESS
You must have made a lengthy study.

FOOL *(nodding)*
Words can change the world.

DUCHESS
So you have said before. I remain unconvinced. Strong men change the world. Strong men and their deeds. Words are like marzipan on the cake. Of course *you* think words are important. You are weak, and have nothing else.

FOOL
Your ladyship is wrong.

DUCHESS *(icily)*
You had better be able to substantiate that comment.

FOOL
Lady, the Duke wishes to chop down the forests, is this not so?

DUKE
The trees talk about me. I hear them whisper when I go riding. They tell lies about me!

(The Fool and the Duchess exchange glances)

FOOL
But this policy has met with fanatical opposition.

DUKE
What?

FOOL
People don't like it.

DUCHESS
What does that matter? We rule! They will do what we say or they will be pitilessly executed!

DUKE
But, my love, we will run out of people!

FOOL
No need, no need! You don't have to do that! What you do is . . . you . . . you embark upon a far-reaching and ambitious plan to expand the agricultural industry, provide long-term employment in the sawmills, open new land for development, and reduce the scope for banditry.

DUKE *(baffled)*
How will I do all that?

FOOL
Chop down the forests.

DUKE
But you said . . .

DUCHESS

Shut up, Felmet. *(she turns to the Fool)* Exactly how does one go about knocking over the houses of people one does not like?

FOOL

Urban clearance.

DUCHESS

I was thinking of burning them down.

FOOL

Hygienic urban clearance.

DUCHESS

And sowing the ground with salt.

FOOL

Marry, I suspect that it is hygienic urban clearance and a programme of environmental improvements. It might be a good idea to plant a few trees as well.

DUKE *(shouting)*

No more trees!

FOOL

Oh, it's all right. They won't survive. The important thing is to have planted them.

DUCHESS

But I also want to raise taxes.

FOOL
  Why, nuncle —

DUCHESS
  And I am not your nuncle.

FOOL
  N'aunt?

DUCHESS
  No.

FOOL
  Why . . . prithee . . . you need to finance your ambitious
  programme for the country.

DUKE *(getting lost)*
  Sorry?

DUCHESS
  He means that chopping down trees costs money. *(to the
  Fool)* Intriguing, but can your words change the past?

FOOL
  More easily, I think. Because the past is what people
  remember, and memories are words. Who knows how a
  king behaved a thousand years ago? There is only recollection, and stories. And plays, of course.

DUKE

Ah yes. I saw a play once. Bunch of funny fellows in tights. A lot of shouting. The people liked it. But you say history is what people are told?

FOOL *(taking a coin from his pocket)*

What about him? Champot the Good. Was he? Who knows, now? What was he good at? But he will be Champot the Good until the end of the world.

DUKE

I want to be a good ruler. I want people to like me.

DUCHESS *(ignoring him)*

Let us assume that there were other matters subject to controversy. Matters of historical record that had . . . been clouded.

DUKE

I didn't do it, you know. He slipped and fell. That was it. He attacked me. It was self-defence. That's it. He slipped and fell on his own dagger in self-defence. I have no recollection of it at this time.

DUCHESS

Be quiet, husband. I know you didn't do it. I wasn't there with you, you may recall. It was I who didn't hand you the dagger. *(turns to the Fool)* And now, Fool. I was saying, I believe, that perhaps there are matters that should be properly recorded.

FOOL

Marry, that you were not there at the time?

DUCHESS

Not where?

FOOL *(hastily)*

Anywhere.

DUCHESS

So long as you remember it. Reality is only weak words, you say. Therefore, words are reality. But how can words become history?

DUKE

It was a very good play I saw. There were fights, and no-one really died. Some very good speeches, I thought.

DUCHESS

Fool?

FOOL

Lady?

DUCHESS

Can you write a play? A play that will go around the world, a play that will be remembered long after rumour has died?

FOOL

No, lady. It is a special talent.

DUCHESS

But can you find someone who has it?

FOOL

There are such people, my lady, in Ankh-Morpork may-hap.

DUCHESS

Find one. Find the best. The truth will out. Find one.

(Lights out)

SCENE 13 – THE BLASTED HEATH

(Magrat, Granny and Nanny are on stage)

GRANNY
We ain't going to curse anyone. It hardly ever works if they done know you've done it.

NANNY
What you do is, you send him a doll of himself with pins in it —

GRANNY
No, Gytha.

NANNY
All you have to do is get hold of some of his toenails.

GRANNY
No.

NANNY
Or some of his hair or anything. I've got some pins.

GRANNY
No.

MAGRAT
Cursing people is morally unsound and extremely bad for your karma.

NANNY
Well, I'm going to curse him, anyway. Under my breath, like. I could've caught my death in that dungeon for all he cared.

GRANNY
We ain't going to curse him, we're going to replace him. What did you do with the old king?

MAGRAT
But you can't put the old king back on the throne. Ghosts can't rule. You'd never get the crown to stay on. It'd drop through.

GRANNY
We're going to replace him with Verence's son. Proper succession.

NANNY
Oh, we've been through all that. In about fifteen years' time, perhaps, but . . .

GRANNY
Tonight.

NANNY
A child on the throne? He wouldn't last five minutes.

GRANNY *(quietly)*
Not a child. A grown man. Remember Aliss Demurrage?

(A pause)

NANNY
Bloody hell. You ain't going to try that, are you?

GRANNY
I mean to have a go.

NANNY
See here, Esme. I mean, Black Aliss was one of the best.
I mean, you're very good at, well, headology and think-
ing and that, but . . .

GRANNY
You're saying I couldn't do it, aren't you?

MAGRAT
Excuse me. Who was Black Aliss? And none of this
exchanging meaningful glances and talking over my
head. There's three of us in this coven, remember?

NANNY
She was before your time. Before mine, really. Lived
over Skund way. Very powerful witch. She turned a
pumpkin into a coach once.

GRANNY

Showy. That's no help to anyone, turning up at a ball smelling like a pie. And that business with the glass slipper. Dangerous, to my mind.

NANNY *(ignoring this interruption)*

But the biggest thing she ever did was to send a whole palace to sleep for a hundred years until . . . Can't remember. Was there rose bushes involved, or was it spinning wheels in that one? I think some princess had to finger . . . no, there was a prince. That was it.

MAGRAT *(uneasily)*

Finger a prince?

NANNY

No, he had to kiss her. Very romantic, Black Aliss was. She liked nothing better than Girl meets Frog.

MAGRAT

Why did they call her Black Aliss?

GRANNY

Fingernails.

NANNY

And teeth. She had a sweet tooth. Lived in a real gingerbread cottage. Couple of kids shoved her in her own oven at the end. Shocking.

MAGRAT

And you're going to send the castle to sleep?

GRANNY

She never sent the castle to sleep. That's just an old wives' tale. *(she glares at Nanny)* She just stirred up time a little. It's not as hard as people think. Everyone does it all the time. It's like rubber, is time. You can stretch it to suit yourself.

MAGRAT

But time is time. Every second lasts a second, that's what they're for . . .

GRANNY

How many times have weeks flown past, when afternoons seem to last for ever? How many times have minutes seemed to last for hours, when some hours have gone so quickly. . . ?

MAGRAT

But that's just people's perception. Isn't it?

GRANNY

Oh yes. Of course it is. It all is. But what difference does that make? I reckon fifteen years would be a nice round number. That means the lad will be eighteen at the finish. We just do the spell, go and fetch him, he can manifest his destiny, and everything will be nice and neat.

NANNY

Could work out nice. A bit of peace and quiet for fifteen years. If I recall the spell, after you say it you have to fly round the castle before cock crow.

GRANNY
I wasn't thinking about that. It wouldn't be right. Felmet would still be king all the time. The kingdom would still get sick. No, what I was thinking of was moving the whole kingdom. *(she beams at them)*

NANNY
The whole of Lancre?

GRANNY
Yes.

NANNY
Fifteen years into the future?

GRANNY
Yes.

NANNY *(looking at Granny's broomstick)*
You'll never do it. Not round the whole kingdom in that, on your own.

GRANNY
I've thought of that. I'm going to need some help. *(she looks pointedly at Nanny)*

NANNY
Bleeding bloody hell!

(Lights out)

94

SCENE 14 – THE WOOD

(Crows caw in the background. Magrat and Fool (wearing a flower pinned to his motley) enter, strolling together, to centre)

MAGRAT
You've been a Fool long?

FOOL *(bitterly)*
All my life. I cut my teeth on a set of bells.

MAGRAT
I suppose it gets handed on, father to son?

FOOL
I never saw much of my father. He went off to be a Fool for the Lords of Quirm when I was small.

MAGRAT
That's terrible. Still, it must be a happy life. Making people laugh, I mean.

FOOL
No. It's a terribly serious business. The College of Fools in Ankh-Morpork is one of the dullest, strictest, most spartan colleges on the whole of Discworld.

MAGRAT
Didn't you want to be anything else?

FOOL
What else is there? I haven't seen anything else I could be. How did you get to be a witch? I mean, did you go to a school or something?

MAGRAT
Oh, no. Goody Whemper just walked down to the village one day, got all us girls lined up, and chose me. You don't choose the Craft, you see. It chooses you.

FOOL
Yes. But when do you actually become a witch?

MAGRAT
When the other witches treat you as one, I suppose. If they ever do. I thought they would after that spell in the corridor. It was pretty good, after all.

FOOL
Marry, it was a rite of passage. Sorry. Er, the other witches being those two old ladies?

MAGRAT
Yes.

FOOL
Very strong characters, I imagine.

MAGRAT
Very. They're quite nice, really. It's just that, well, when you're a witch you don't think about other people. I mean you think about them, but you don't actually think about their feelings, if you see what I mean.

FOOL
You're not like that.

MAGRAT
Look, I wish you'd stop working for the Duke. You know what he's like. Torturing people and setting fire to their cottages.

FOOL
But I'm his Fool. Right until he dies. I'm afraid it's tradition. Tradition is very important.

MAGRAT
You don't even like being a Fool . . .

FOOL
I hate it. But if I've got to be one, I may as well do it properly.

MAGRAT
That's really stupid!

FOOL
Foolish, I prefer. *(pause)* If I kiss you, do I turn into a frog?

(As they kiss, they freeze. Lights up on another part of the stage – preferably higher than the Fool and Magrat, where Nanny and Granny are saying the spell)

GRANNY

By the infinite might of the all powerful Great A'Tuin, the star turtle who supports our Discworld, and by the four great elephants who stand upon his meteor-pocked back and hold the world on their mighty shoulders, I conjure the gods of Fate, Destiny and Time. The Kingdom of Lancre shall remain frozen while the whole of Discworld moves on fifteen years full and final. Then shall nemesis come to Felmet self-styled king of Lancre.

Right, we're off!

(They grab their broomsticks and start to exit)

NANNY

Does yours still need to be bump-started?

GRANNY

I'm afraid so.

(And they are gone) [Magic effect. We used stage flashes, a disco wheel and a gobo of a witch on a broomstick, flying around the stage, all to the accompaniment of 'The Ride of the Valkyries']

INTERVAL

[NOTE – The scene continues after the interval. The lights come up on the frozen pair, who now break from their kiss]

FOOL
Did you feel the whole world move?

MAGRAT *(to herself)*
They've done it. We kissed for fifteen years.

FOOL
What?

MAGRAT
She's done it!

FOOL
Done what?

MAGRAT
Oh. Nothing. Nothing much, really.

FOOL
Shall we try that again? It would be something to remember on my long journey to Ankh-Morpork.

MAGRAT
What! That's five hundred miles away! You'll be away for ages!

FOOL

I can't help it. The Duke's given me special instructions. To get a playwright...

MAGRAT

But you don't have to go. You don't want to go!

FOOL

That doesn't have very much to do with it. I promised to be loyal to him...

MAGRAT

Yes, yes, until you're dead! But you don't believe that!

FOOL

Well, yes. But I still have to do it. I gave my word.

MAGRAT

Just when we were getting to know each other! You're pathetic!

FOOL

I'd only be pathetic if I broke my word. But I may be incredibly ill-advised. I'm sorry. I'll be back in a few weeks anyway.

MAGRAT

Don't you understand I'm asking you not to listen to him?

FOOL
I said I'm sorry. I couldn't see you again before I go, could I?

MAGRAT *(stiffly)*
I shall be washing my hair.

FOOL
When?

MAGRAT
Whenever!

(Lights out)

SCENE 15 – A STREET IN
ANKH-MORPORK

(On stage are three robbers, around the Fool, who is on the ground. Tomjon and Hwel enter)

TOMJON
  What's this?

HWEL
  It's a clown! They're mugging a clown!

(As they reach the others, the leader holds up a business card)

TOMJON
  'Theft Licence'?

ROBBER 1
  That's right, only don't expect us to do you too, 'cos we're on our way home.

ROBBER 2
  That's right. We've done our whoosit, quota.

HWEL
  But you were kicking him!

ROBBER 1
  Werl, not a lot. Not what you'd call actual kicking.

ROBBER 3
More what you'd call foot-nudging, sort of thing. *(He demonstrates)*

TOMJON
Well, it all seems to be in order.

HWEL *(who is helping Fool up)*
In order? To rob someone?

ROBBER 1
We'll give him a chitty, of course. So he won't get done again today.

TOMJON
How much did you get?

ROBBER 1 *(opens Fool's purse)*
Oh, bloody hell. *(He shows the other robbers)*

ROBBER 2
Now we're for it.

ROBBER 1
Well, how was I to know? I mean, look at him; how much would you expect him to be carrying? Couple of coppers, right? I mean, we'd never have done him, only it was on our way home. You try to do someone a favour and this is what happens.

TOMJON
How much has he got then?

ROBBER 1 *(fed up)*
There must be a hundred silver dollars in here. I mean, that's not in our league. You've got to be in the Guild of Solicitors or something to steal that much. It's way over our quota.

TOMJON
Give it back, then.

ROBBER 1
But we've given him a receipt.

ROBBER 2
They've all got numbers on. The Guild of Thieves check up on them . . .

TOMJON
How would it be, then, if you were to rob him of, say, five copper pieces, instead.

FOOL
Here, what's going on?

TOMJON
That represents two copper pieces as the going rate, plus expenses of three copper pieces for time, call-out fees . . .

ROBBER 1
Wear and tear on cosh.

TOMJON
Exactly.

ROBBER 1
Very fair, very fair. *(takes the coins out of the purse. Gives the rest back to Tomjon)* Come on then, lads.

(They all exit)

FOOL
That was amazing. How can I thank you, sir?

HWEL
You're a Fool, aren't you?

FOOL
Yes. It's the bells, isn't it? Well, I'm really grateful. Is there a tavern around here, I'd like to buy you boys a drink.

TOMJON
Well, that would be . . .

HWEL
We'd love to, but we need to get back to the theatre.

FOOL
You two are in the theatre?

HWEL
That's right. This here is Tomjon, son of the great Vitoller. I am Hwel, the playwright.

FOOL

Then I've come five hundred miles to find you. *(he links arms with them, and they start to exit)*

(Lights out)

SCENE 16 – THE THEATRE

(Vitoller, Tomjon and Hwel are on stage)

VITOLLER
Can you do it?

TOMJON
It sounded interesting, the way he told it. Wicked king ruling with the help of evil witches. Storms. Ghastly forests. True Heir to the Throne in life and death struggle. Flash of dagger. Screams, alarums. Evil king dies. Good triumphs. Bells ring out.

VITOLLER
Showers of rose petals could be arranged. I know a man who can get them practically at cost.

(He and Tomjon look at Hwel. All three turn and look at the Fool's bag of gold, on the table)

You'll do it then, will you?

HWEL
It's got a certain something. But, I don't know . . .

VITOLLER
I'm not trying to pressure you, you know.

(They all turn again and look at the gold)

TOMJON
It seems a bit fishy. I mean the Fool is decent enough. But the way he tells it . . . it's very odd. His mouth says the words, and his eyes say something else. And I got the impression he'd much rather we believed his eyes.

VITOLLER
On the other hand, what harm can it do? The pay's the thing. Er, play. . . the play's the thing.

HWEL
But we can already afford to build the Dysk Theatre.

VITOLLER
Just the shell and the stage. But not all the other things. Not the trapdoor mechanism, or the machine for lowering gods out of heaven. Or the big turntable, or the wind fans.

HWEL
We used to manage without all that stuff. Remember the old days? All we had was a few planks and a bit of painted sacking. But we had a lot of spirit. Mind you, we could afford a wave machine. A small one. I've got this idea about this ship wrecked on this island . . .

VITOLLER (shaking his head)
Sorry.

TOMJON
But we've had some huge audiences!

VITOLLER

Yes, but they pay in halfpennies. I already owe Chrystophrase the Troll more than I should.

TOMJON

But he's the one who has people's limbs torn off!

HWEL

How much do you owe him?

VITOLLER

It's all right, I'm keeping up the interest payments. More or less.

HWEL

Yes, but how much does he want?

VITOLLER

An arm and a leg.

HWEL *and* TOMJON

What??

VITOLLER

I did it for you two! Tomjon deserves a better stage. He doesn't want to go ruining his health sleeping in lattys and never knowing a home. And you, my man, you need somewhere settled, with all the proper things you ought to have . . . like trapdoors and . . . wave machines and so forth.

You talked me into building the Dysk Theatre, and I thought, they're right. It's no life on the road, giving two performances a day to a bunch of farmers and going round with the hat afterwards, what sort of future is that? We need our own place, with comfortable seats for the gentry people who don't throw potatoes on the stage. I said, blow the cost. I just wanted you to—

HWEL

All right! All right, I'll write it!

TOMJON

I'll act it.

VITOLLER

I'm not forcing you, mind. It's your own choice.

HWEL

Mind you, there were some nice touches. The three witches was good. Lots of smoke and green light. You could do a lot with three witches. Surprising no-one's thought of it before, really.

VITOLLER

So we can tell this Fool that we'll do it, can we?

HWEL

And of course you couldn't go wrong with a good storm. And there was that ghost routine we cut out of 'Please Yourself' 'cos we couldn't afford the muslin. P'raps I could put Death in, too.

TOMJON

How far away did he say he came from?

VITOLLER
The Ramtops. Some little kingdom no-one has ever heard of. It'd take months to get there.

TOMJON
I'd like to go, anyway. That's where I was born.

(Vitoller looks at the ceiling, Hwel looks at the floor)

That's what you said, when you were on a tour of the mountains.

VITOLLER
Yes, but I can't remember where.

TOMJON
I could take some of the younger lads and we could make a summer of it.

VITOLLER
Hwel's got to write the play, yet.

(But he has already started. They exchange glances, then quietly leave him to it)

(Lights out)

SCENE 17 – THE THEATRE

(Exactly as for Scene 16, but the following day. Vitoller and Hwel are on stage. Vitoller has just finished reading Hwel's play)

VITOLLER
It's a good play. Apart from the ghost.

HWEL *(sullenly)*
The ghost stays.

VITOLLER
But people always jeer and throw things. Anyway, you know how hard it is to get all the chalk out of the clothes.

HWEL *(defensively)*
I like ghosts.

VITOLLER
You still bent on going?

HWEL
Yes. Tomjon's still a bit wild. He needs an older head around the place.

VITOLLER

I'll miss you, laddie, I don't mind telling you. You've been like a son to me. How old are you, exactly? I never did know.

HWEL

Fifty-eight.

VITOLLER

You've been like an older brother to me, then. I don't know what I'll do without you and Tomjon around, and that's a fact.

HWEL

It's only for the summer. You said yourself it'd be a good experience.

VITOLLER

We grow old, Master Hwel.

HWEL

Aye. You don't want him to go, do you?

VITOLLER

I was all for it at first. You know. Then I thought, there's destiny afoot. Just when things are going well, there's always bloody destiny. I mean, that's where he came from somewhere in the mountains. Now fate is calling him back. I shan't see him again.

HWEL

It's only for the summer...

VITOLLER *(holding up a hand)*
Don't interrupt. I'd got the right dramatic flow there.

HWEL
Sorry.

VITOLLER
I mean, you know he's not my flesh and blood.

HWEL
He's your son, though. This heredity business isn't all it's cracked up to be.

VITOLLER
But you said he looks like this Fool person. I can't see it myself, mark you.

HWEL
The light's got to be right.

VITOLLER
Could be some destiny at work there, too.

(Lights out)

SCENE 18 – WITCH'S HOUSE

(Granny, Nanny and Magrat are on stage)

GRANNY *(squinting into a crystal ball)*
He's definitely on his way. In a cart.

NANNY
A fiery white charger would have been favourite.

MAGRAT
Has he got a magic sword?

GRANNY
You're a disgrace, the pair of you.

MAGRAT
A magic sword is important. We could make him one, out of thunderbolt iron. I've got a spell for that. You take some thunderbolt iron . . . and then you make a sword out of it.

GRANNY
I can't be having with that old stuff.

NANNY
And a strawberry birthmark.

GRANNY

Can't abide strawberries. It must have worked. Otherwise he wouldn't be coming here. I dare say the armour and the swords are in the carts.

NANNY

It's a long road. There's many a slip twixt dress and drawers. There could be bandits.

GRANNY

We shall watch over him.

MAGRAT

That's not right. If he's going to be king he ought to be able to fight his own battles.

NANNY

We don't want him to go wasting his strength. We want him good and fresh when he gets here.

MAGRAT

And then I hope we shall leave him to fight his battles in his own way.

GRANNY

Quite right. Provided he looks like winning. *(she exits)*

MAGRAT

Whatever happened to not meddling?

NANNY

It's not proper meddling. Just helping matters along.

MAGRAT

But only last week you were saying . . .

NANNY

A week is a long time in magic. Fifteen years, for one thing. Anyway, Esme is determined and I'm in no mood to stop her.

MAGRAT

So what you're saying is that 'not meddling' is like taking a vow not to swim. You'll absolutely never break it unless of course you happen to find yourself in the water?

NANNY

It's better than drowning.

MAGRAT

I think that I shall never really understand about witch-craft. Just when I think I've got a grip on it, it changes.

NANNY

We're all just people. *(a new thought)* Had a row with your young man?

MAGRAT

I really don't know what you're talking about.

NANNY

Haven't seen him about for weeks.

MAGRAT

Oh, the Duke sent him to . . . sent him away for something or another. Not that it bothers me at all. Either way.

NANNY *(sarcastically)*

Oh, quite.

(Lights out)

SCENE 19 – ON THE ROAD

(Tomjon, Hwel and Players)

TOMJON *(examining a map)*
I think we're lost.

HWEL
We were lost ten miles ago. There's got to be a new word
for what we are now.

TOMJON
Where are we, then?

HWEL
The mountains. Perfectly clear on my atlas.

TOMJON
We ought to stop and ask someone.

HWEL
A lonely curlew? A badger? Who did you have in mind?

TOMJON *(pointing off)*
That old woman in the funny hat. I've been watching
her. She keeps ducking down behind a bush when she
thinks I've seen her.

HWEL
Ho there, good mother!

GRANNY *(off)*
Whose mother?

HWEL
Just a figure of speech, Mrs . . . Miss . . .

GRANNY *(entering)*
Mistress! *(defiantly)* And I'm a poor old woman gathering wood. Lawks! You did give me a fright, young master. My poor old heart!

TOMJON
I'm sorry?

GRANNY
What?

TOMJON
Your poor old heart what?

GRANNY
What about my poor old heart?

HWEL
It's just that you mentioned it.

GRANNY
Well, it isn't important. Lawks. I expect you're looking for Lancre.

TOMJON
    Well, yes. All day.

GRANNY
    You've come too far. Go back about two miles, and take
    the track on the right, past the stand of pines.

PLAYER *(tugging at Tomjon's sleeve)*
    When you m-meet a m-mysterious old lady in the road,
    you've got to offer to sh-share your lunch, or help her
    across the river.

TOMJON
    You have?

PLAYER
    It's t-terribly b-bad luck not to.

TOMJON *(to Granny)*
    Would you care to share our lunch, good mo— old
    wo— ma'am?

GRANNY
    What is it?

TOMJON
    Salt pork.

GRANNY *(shaking her head)*
    Thanks all the same. But it gives me wind. *(She turns on
    her heel and sets off up the road)*

TOMJON *(calling after her)*
We could help you across the river if you like!

HWEL
What river? We're on the moors, there can't be a river for miles.

PLAYER
Y-you've got to get them on y-your side.

HWEL
Perhaps we should have asked her to wait while we went and looked for one! Come on!

(They start to exit)

(Lights out)

SCENE 20 – THE WOODS

(The Fool is onstage. Magrat enters, in a foul temper)

MAGRAT
What's all this about a play?

FOOL *(sagging)*
Aren't you glad to see me?

MAGRAT
Well, yes. Of course. Now, this play . . .

FOOL
My lord wants something to convince people that he is the rightful King of Lancre. Himself mostly, I think.

MAGRAT
Is that why you went to Ankh-Morpork?

FOOL
Yes.

MAGRAT
It's disgusting!

FOOL
You would prefer the Duchess's approach? She just thinks they ought to kill everyone. She's good at that sort

of thing. And then there'd be fighting and everything. Lots of people would die anyway. This way might be easier.

MAGRAT

Oh, where's your spunk, man?

FOOL

Pardon?

MAGRAT

Don't you want to die nobly for a just cause?

FOOL

I'd much rather live quietly for one. It's all right for you witches, you can do what you like, but I'm circumscribed.

MAGRAT *(over-casually)*

When's this play going to be, then?

FOOL

Marry, I'm sure I'm not allowed to tell you. The Duke said to me, he said, don't tell the witches that it's tomorrow night.

MAGRAT

I shouldn't then.

FOOL

At eight o'clock.

MAGRAT
I see.

FOOL
But meet for sherry beforehand at seven-thirty, i'faith.

MAGRAT
I expect you shouldn't tell me who is invited, either.

FOOL
That's right. Most of the dignitaries of Lancre. You understand I'm not telling you all this?

MAGRAT
That's right.

FOOL
But I think you have a right to know what it is you're not being told.

MAGRAT
Good point. Is there still that little gate around the back, that leads to the kitchens?

FOOL
The one that often gets left unguarded?

MAGRAT
Yes.

FOOL

Oh, we hardly ever guard it these days.

MAGRAT

Do you think there might be someone guarding it at around eight o'clock tomorrow?

FOOL

Well, I might be there.

MAGRAT

Good.

FOOL

The Duke will be expecting you.

MAGRAT

You said he said we weren't to know.

FOOL

He said I mustn't tell you. But he also said, 'They'll come anyway. I hope they do.' Strange, he seemed in a very good mood when he said it. Can I see you after the show?

MAGRAT

I think I might be washing my hair. Excuse me, but I think I ought to be going.

(She starts to leave)

FOOL

Yes, but I brought you this pres — *(but she has gone)* Ah, well. Marry, 'tis true, witches sometimes do unpleasant things to people, sometimes.

(Lights out)

SCENE 21 – THE MAIN HALL OF THE - CASTLE

(The Play. The action alternates between the auditorium (- played by us in an on–stage balcony; a rostrum to one side of the stage would also suffice) and backstage (played on the main stage). Throughout, we hear, indistinctly, the action of the play continuing 'off-stage')

AUDITORIUM

(The Fool, and some guests, are on stage. The three witches enter with Verence)

FOOL
There's not going to be any trouble, is there? I don't want there to be any trouble. Please.

GRANNY *(regally)*
I'm sure I don't know h— what you mean.

NANNY
Wotcha, jingle bells! I hope you haven't been keeping our girl here up late o'nights!

MAGRAT
Nanny!

(They seat themselves)

NANNY *(to Granny, offering a walnut)*
Want one?

(Granny shakes her head)

(To Verence) Walnut?

VERENCE
No, thank you. They go right through me, you know.

ACTOR *(off)*
Come, gentles, all and list to our tale . . . *(he continues, indistinctly during the dialogue)*

GRANNY
What's this? Who's the fellow in the tights?

NANNY
He's the Prologue. You have to have him in the beginning so everyone knows what the play's about.

GRANNY
Can't understand a word. What's a gentle, anyway?

NANNY
Type of maggot.

GRANNY
That's nice, isn't it? 'Hello, maggots, welcome to the show'. Puts people in a nice frame of mind, doesn't it?

NANNY
  These walnuts are damn tough. I'm going to have to take
  my boot off to this one . . .

BACKSTAGE

(*Hwel is looking off, onto the stage, at the show. He is carrying a small cauldron*)

HWEL
  C'mon, Come on! *(prompting)* 'What hath befell the
  land?' *(he turns)* And where are the witches? Where are
  the blasted witches??

(*Three unlikely-looking witches enter*)

WITCH 1
  I've lost my wart!

WITCH 2
  The cauldron's all full of yuk!

WITCH 3
  There's something living in this wig!

HWEL
  Calm down, calm down! It'll be all right on the night!

WITCH 1
  This is the night, Hwel!

(*Hwel hears a pause on stage, he prompts*)

HWEL
'avenge the terror of thy father's death.' *(He turns to the 'witches' and starts to psyche them up, in the manner of an American sports coach)* Right, Now what are you? You're evil hags, right?

WITCHES
Yes, Hwel.

HWEL
Tell me what you are.

WITCHES
We're evil hags, Hwel.

HWEL
Louder!

WITCHES
We're evil hags!

HWEL
And what are you going to do?

WITCH 2 *(uncertainly)*
We're going to curse people . . . ?

HWEL
I can't hear you!

WITCHES
We're going to curse people!

HWEL
What are you?

WITCHES
We're hags, Hwel!

HWEL
What sort of hags?

WITCHES
We're black and midnight hags!

HWEL
Are you scheming?

WITCHES
Yeah!

HWEL
Are you secret?

WITCHES
Yeah!

HWEL
What are you?

WITCHES
We're scheming evil secret black and midnight hags!

HWEL
Right! Now I want you to get out there and give 'em hell. *(He absent-mindedly puts the cauldron on his head, in the manner of, say, John Wayne in any one of half-a-dozen WW2 movies and looks out front. He adopts an American accent)* Not for me . . . not for the goddam captain . . . but for Corporal Walkowski and his little dawg. *(He pushes the rim of the helmet up with his thumb. A pause. He snaps out of his reverie)* What are you waiting for? Get out there and curse them!

(They exit)

TOMJON *(entering)*
Hwel, there's no crown. I've got to wear a crown.

HWEL
Of course there's a crown. The big one with the red glass, very impressive, we used it in that place with the big square . . .

TOMJON
I think we left it there.

(Hwel judges another prompt is needed)

HWEL
'I have smothered many a babe . . .' *(to Tomjon)* Well, just find another one, then. In the props box. You're the evil King Verence, you've got to have a crown. Improvise . . .

GRANNY

Gytha.

NANNY

I never shipwrecked anybody! They just said they ship-wreck people! I never did!

MAGRAT

Green blusher! *(to Fool)* I don't look like that, do I?

FOOL

Absolutely not.

VERENCE

That's him, isn't it? That's my son! But what is he doing? What is he saying?

NANNY

I think he's meant to be you.

VERENCE

But I never walked like that! Why's he got a hump on his back? What's happened to his leg? *(pause)* And I certainly never did that! Or that. Why is he saying that I did?

(Nanny shrugs)

And it's my crown he's wearing! Look! This is it! And he's saying I did all those . . . All right. Maybe I did that.

So I set fire to few cottages. Everyone does that. It's good for the building industry, anyway. Why is he saying all this about me?

NANNY

It's art. It holds a wossname, mirror, up to life. That's us. Round that silly cauldron. That's meant to be us.

GRANNY

Bloody distorted one at that. But the audience are taken in: it's more real than reality. It's not true, but that has nothing to do with it. Words. As soft as water, and as powerful as water, too, carrying away the past. We've lost. There's nothing we can do against this.

NANNY

Did you hear that? One of them said they put babies in their cauldron! I'm not sitting here listening to these lies!

GRANNY

Don't do anything! It'll make things worse! Words. That's all that's left. Words.

NANNY

And now there's a man with a trumpet come on. What's he going to do?

(Trumpet effect, off)

Oh. End of Act One.

(Sound of applause)

135

VERENCE

My own flesh and blood. Why has he done this to me?

GRANNY

Come, Gytha, we're going backstage.

(The witches and Verence exit, with the Fool)

(The Duke enters. His hands are now covered in bloody bandages. He scratches away under the bandages with a large knitting needle – if this doesn't get your audience squirming in their seats . . . well, you've had your chance and muffed it!)

DUKE

Guards, go, find the witches and arrest them.

DUCHESS

Remember what happened last time, foolish man.

DUKE

We left two of them loose. This time . . . all three. The tide of public feeling is on our side. That sort of thing affects witches, depend upon it. You must admit, my precious, that the play seems to be having the desired effect.

DUCHESS

It would appear so.

DUKE *(turning to the guards again)*
Very well. Don't just stand there. Before the play ends, those witches are to be under lock and key.

BACKSTAGE

WIMSLOE *(who is dressed as Death)*
Cower now, Brief Mortals. For I am Death, 'gainst whom no . . . no . . . no . . . Hwel – 'gainst whom no?

HWEL
Oh, good grief, Wimsloe . . . 'Gainst whom no lock will hold nor fasten'd portal bar'. I really don't see why you have difficulty with it. *(he exits)*

WIMSLOE
Right. 'Gainst whom no . . . tumpty-tum . . . nor tumpty-tumpty bar.

(Tomjon enters)

Do you think I'm fearsome enough?

TOMJON
No problem, my friend. Compared with a visit from you, even Death himself would hold no fears.

WIMSLOE
Great. Thanks, Tomjon. *(he exits)*

TOMJON

The play's just not working. It keeps trying to force itself
into different words. It's not right. Once it's written, a
play should just stay writ. It shouldn't come alive and
start twisting itself around. No wonder everyone needs
prompting all the time. *(he exits)*

(The witch actors enter, escorted by guards)

WITCH 1

But we're not witches!

GUARD

Why do you look like them, then? Tie their hands.

WITCH 2

Yes, but excuse me, we're not really witches!

GUARD 2

Shall we gag them as well?

WITCH 3

If you'd just listen, we're with the theatre —

GUARD

Yes, gag them. Very well then, my theatrical witches.
You've done your show, and now it's time for your
applause. *Clap* them in irons! *(he laughs ironically)*

(The guards drag them off. The real witches enter)

GRANNY *(reading a script)*
'Divers alarums and excursions'?

MAGRAT
That means lots of terrible happenings. You always put that in plays. We can't let this happen. If this gets about, witches will always be old hags in green blusher. Witches just aren't like that. Why don't we just change the words?

GRANNY
I suppose you're an expert at theatre words? They'd have to be the proper sort, or people'd suspect.

NANNY
I don't know about new words. But we can make them forget these words.

GRANNY
I suppose it's worth a try.

(Hwel enters)

HWEL
At last! What are you three playing at? We've been looking for you everywhere!

MAGRAT
Us? But we're not . . .

HWEL

Oh yes, you are! We put it in last week, remember? You don't need to say anything, you just sit there and symbolise occult forces at work. Come on, you've done well so far. *(he slaps Magrat on the bottom)* Good complexion you've got there, Wilph. You look as nasty a bunch of hags as a body might hope to clap eyes on. Well done. Pity about the wigs. Curtain up in one minute. Break a leg. *(He slaps Magrat on the bottom again, and hurries off)*

GRANNY

Useful.

NANNY *in Hwel's direction)*

Break your own leg. *(There is a cry of pain)* Come on, girls. *(They exit)*

(NOTE – Hwel should limp when he next appears on-stage!)

(Lights out)

SCENE 22 – ON STAGE

(The Play. To one side of the stage at the front are two chairs, on which are sat the real Duke and Duchess. On 'stage' are Tomjon, as 'bad' King Verence (looking a lot like Richard III,) Bedlin as 'good' Duke Felmet, and Gumridge as Lady Felmet. All three stand amazed as Granny, Nanny and Magrat take up their places)

HWEL *(off)*
Get on with it!

BEDLIN
And now our domination is complete...

NANNY *(tapping the cauldron)*
It's just tin, this one.

MAGRAT
And the fire is just red paper.

GRANNY
Never mind. Just look busy, and wait till I say.

BEDLIN
The very soil cries out at tyranny . . . erm.

TOMJON *(prompting)*
And calls me forth for vengeance.

BEDLIN *(pointing at the witches)*
B–but...

MAGRAT
How do they make it flicker?

TOMJON *(prompting Bedlin again)*
And calls me forth for vengeance...

GRANNY
Be quiet, you two. You're upsetting people. Go ahead, young man. Don't mind us.

BEDLIN
Wha...?

TOMJON *(desperately)*
Aha, it calls you forth for vengeance, does it? And the heavens cry revenge, too, I expect.

DUKE *(cowering in his seat)*
There they are. That's them. What are they doing in my play?

TOMJON
Aha, thou callst me an evil king, though thou whisperest it so none save I may hear it. And thou hast summoned the guard, possibly by some secret signal, owing naught to artifice of lips or tongue.

(A 'guard' enters, crabwise, and hisses at Tomjon)

'GUARD'
Hwel says what the hell is going on?

TOMJON
What was that? Did I hear you say, 'I come, my lady'?

'GUARD'
Get these people off, he says.

TOMJON *(ignoring him)*
Thou babblest, man. See how I dodge thy tortoise spear. I said, see how I dodge thy tortoise spear. Thy spear, man. You're holding it in thy bloody hand, for goodness' sake.

(There is a desperate silence. Granny walks to the front of the 'stage')

GRANNY
Ghost of the mind and all device away, I bid the Truth to have . . . its tumpty-tumpty day.

(She returns to her place on stage. Hwel enters during the following dialogue)

GUMRIDGE *(the words are forming themselves in his mouth)*
Do you fear him now? And he so mazed with drink? Take his dagger, husband . . . you are a blade's width from the kingdom.

BEDLIN

I dare not.

GUMRIDGE

Who will know? See, there is only the eyeless night. Take the dagger now, take the kingdom tomorrow. Have a stab at it, man.

BEDLIN

I have it, wife. Is this a dagger I see before me?

GUMRIDGE

Of course it's a bloody dagger. Come on, do it now. The weak deserve no mercy. We'll say he fell downstairs.

BEDLIN

I cannot! He has been kindness itself to me.

GUMRIDGE

And you can be Death itself to him . . .

BEDLIN

No, I cannot do it! I will be seen! Down there in the hall, someone watches!

GUMRIDGE

There is no-one! Must I put it in for you? See, his foot is on the stair . . .

DUKE *(rushing on to the stage)*
No! I did not do it! It was not like that! You were not there! *(he looks around)* Nor was I! *(giggles)* I was asleep at the time, you know. There was blood on the counter-pane, blood on the floor. I couldn't wash it off. These are not proper matters for this inquiry. I cannot allow the discussion of national security. It was just a dream . . . When I awoke, he'd be alive tomorrow. And tomorrow you can say I did not know. I had no recollection. What a noise he made in falling. Enough to wake the dead . . . who would have thought he had so much blood in him? . . . *(grins brightly at the assembled company)* I hope that sorts it all out. Ha. Ha.

DUCHESS
These are just slanders. And treason to boot. The rantings of mad players. Therefore there is no proof. And where there is no proof there is no crime.

FOOL *(entering)*
No. I saw it all. I was in the Great Hall that night. You killed the King, my lord.

DUKE
I did not! You were not there! I did not see you there! I order you not to be there! You swore loyalty unto death!

FOOL
Yes, my lord. I'm sorry.

DUKE
You're dead!

(He snatches a knife off Bedlin, and stabs the Fool)

FOOL *(collapsing to the floor)*
Thank goodness that's over.

MAGRAT
Verence! *(she crosses to him)*

DUKE
I didn't do it. You all saw that I didn't do it. Telling lies
is naughty. *(He stabs himself with the knife, and hands it
to Granny Weatherwax)* You can't get me now. *(He starts
to exit.)* Will there be a comet? There must be a comet
when a prince dies.
(he wanders away)

*(Granny walks over to the knife, picks it up and tests the blade.
It retracts back into the handle (or the blade's made of rubber
– whichever you can get!)*

GRANNY
There's your magic sword.

MAGRAT
Are you dead or not? *(she holds him to her bosom)*

FOOL
I must be. I'm in paradise.

MAGRAT
No, look, I'm serious.

FOOL *(checking himself)*
I'm alive.

GRANNY
Of course. It's a trick dagger. Actors can't be trusted with real ones.

DUCHESS
Clearly my husband has lost his wits. I decree—

GRANNY
Be silent, woman! The true King of Lancre stands before you! *(she points at Tomjon)*

TOMJON
Who, me?

DUCHESS
Oh no. We're not having that. No mysterious returned heirs in this kingdom. You don't frighten me, wyrd sisters.

GRANNY
No. We don't, do we? We really don't.

DUCHESS
Your witchcraft is all artifice and illusion, to amaze weak minds. It holds no fears for me. Do your worst.

GRANNY *(after a threatening pause)*
My worst?

DUCHESS
Yes, get on with it! I'm proud of what I've done, do you hear? I enjoyed it, and I did it because I wanted to! *(to the others)* You gawping idiots! You're so weak! There's not one of you that doesn't fear me! I can make you widdle your drawers out of terror, and now I'm going to take—

(Nanny hits her on the head with a rock (or whatever your props people can come up with))

NANNY
She does go on, don't she? Where's the Duke?

GUARD *(entering)*
He fell over the battlements. Eventually.

GRANNY
Take her away and lock her up. And now, my lad. You are the King of Lancre.

TOMJON
But I don't know how to be a king! I don't want to be a king! Listen to me, all of you. I thank you for your offer. It's a great honour. But I can't accept it. I've worn more crowns than you can count, and the only kingdom I know how to rule has got curtains in front of it. I'm sorry.

HWEL *(stepping forward)*
    The problem is that you don't actually have a choice.
    You are the king, you see. It's a job you are lined up for
    when you're born. The only chance you've got is if there
    was another heir. You don't remember any brothers or
    sisters, do you? *(he looks pointedly at the Fool)*

MAGRAT
    Verence!

(They all turn to look at the Fool)

(Lights out)

SCENE 23 – THE BLASTED HEATH AGAIN

(Granny, Nanny and Magrat are on stage)

GRANNY
It was a good banquet, I thought.

NANNY
I got a coronation mug, too. It says, 'Viva Verence II Rex'. Fancy him being called Rex. I can't say it's a good likeness, mind you. I don't recall him having a handle sticking out of his ear.

MAGRAT
What happened to the Duchess?

GRANNY
She escaped from the castle. Didn't get far. Had to go through the forest. The animals got her. That's Destiny for you. Still, we've got a king. And there's an end of it.

MAGRAT
It's thanks to you and Nanny really.

NANNY
Why?

MAGRAT

It's because you spoke up. Everyone knows witches don't lie, that's the important thing. I mean, everyone could see they looked alike, but that could have been coincidence. You see, I looked up 'droit de seigneur'. Goody Whemper had a dictionary.

GRANNY

Yes. Well. Erm.

MAGRAT

You did tell the truth, didn't you? They really are brothers, aren't they?

NANNY

Oh yes. Definitely. I saw to his mother when your . . . when the new king was born. And to the queen when young Tomjon was born, and she told me who the father was.

MAGRAT

Just a minute.

NANNY

I remember the Fool's father. Very personable young man. He didn't get on with his dad, you know. But he used to visit sometimes. To see old friends.

GRANNY

He made friends easily.

NANNY

Among the ladies. Very athletic, wasn't he? Could climb walls like nobody's business. I remember hearing. Very popular with the queen.

GRANNY

The king used to go out hunting such a lot.

NANNY

It was that droit of his. Always out and about with it, he was.

MAGRAT

Just a minute.

GRANNY

Yes?

MAGRAT

You told everyone they were brothers and that Verence was the older.

NANNY

That's right.

MAGRAT

And you let everyone believe that.

GRANNY

We're bound to be truthful. But there's no call to be honest.

MAGRAT

No, no, what you're saying is that the King of Lancre isn't really . . .

GRANNY

What I'm saying is that we've got a king who's got his head screwed on right, and the old king's ghost has been laid to rest happy. There's been an enjoyable coronation and some of us got mugs we weren't entitled to, them being only for kiddies, and, all in all, things are a lot more satisfactory than they might be. Never mind what should be or what might be or what ought to be. It's what things are that's important.

MAGRAT

But he's not really a king!

NANNY

But he might be. The late queen wasn't very good at counting. Anyway, he doesn't know he isn't royalty.

GRANNY

Anyway, look at it this way. Royalty has to start somewhere. It might as well start with him. How are you and he getting on, now, by the way?

MAGRAT *(coyly)*

All right. *(pause)* I'm surprised at you two. I really am. You're witches. That means you have to care about things like truth and destiny, don't you?

GRANNY

That's where you've been getting it all wrong. Destiny is important, but people go wrong when they think it controls them. It's the other way around.

NANNY

Bugger destiny.

GRANNY

After all, you never thought being a witch was going to be easy, did you?

MAGRAT

I'm learning. I think I'd better be off. It's getting early.

NANNY

Me too. Our Shirl frets if I'm not home when she comes to get my breakfast.

GRANNY

When shall we three meet again?

NANNY

I'm a bit busy this month. Birthdays and such. You know.

GRANNY

That's nice. How about you, Magrat?

MAGRAT

There always seems to be such a lot to do at this time of year, don't you find?

GRANNY *(pleasantly)*

Quite. It's no good getting yourself tied down to appointments all the time, is it? Let's just leave the whole question open, shall we?

(They all nod, and start to leave the stage in separate directions)

(Lights out)

[NOTE – in the curtain call, we brought our Fool on wearing the crown on his fool's cap – just in case the audience hadn't got the point!]

THE END

WYRD SISTERS – PROPS LIST

On the furniture side, we just had two thrones (*for the castle scenes*), plus a small table and some multi-purpose chairs (*various witchs' houses, the theatre, etc*). We also scrounged a set of stocks for the dungeon.

Property	Scene Where First Used	Used By
Smouldering Cauldron	1	On Stage
Pocket Diary	1	Granny W
Pocket Diary	1	Nanny O
Basket with Baby and Crown (Plain)	1	Soldier
Crossbow	1	Bowman
Sword	1	Bowman
Dagger	1	2nd Soldier
Grubby Hanky	2	Duke
Drawstring Purse of Coins	3	Granny W
Bladder on a Stick	4	Fool
Mini-Jester's Head on a Stick	4	Fool
Candle and Candlestick	5	On Stage
Sandpaper Block	6	Duke